DEATH AT WINDOVER

A Florida Murder Mystery Novel
Book 1

Second Edition

Jay Heavner

Canaveral Publishing

Death at Windover

by Jay Heavner
Copyright ©2019 Jay Heavner
Canaveral Publishing
ISBN 978-1-7336174-2-0

Author's photo by Jay Heavner
Cover by Fineline Printing & Graphics, Titusville, Florida

Acknowledgment

Thanks to my wife, who encouraged me to start writing and to my friends, readers, and acquaintances that supported and goaded me as I developed as a serious storyteller and writer.

To Marsha Tressler who read the rough and unfinished draft and gave a two thumbs up and JoAnn Peterson, special thanks for her hard work editing and proofing and the special comment that meant so much, "This is the best you have written yet."

To Tom Bradford for his help with the Hebrew prayer.

Also, for all the people in Florida who kept asking for a book on the Sunshine State. We sure have more than our share of strange and unusual characters and true stories to work with that you couldn't make up in a million years.

Dedicated
to
Clara and Madeline

If you'd like to receive my newsletter or drop me a line, you can send that information to me at
jay@jayheavner.com

My newsletter will contain specials, book recommendations, and updates on coming books and events, and anything else that may interest you.

The Braddock's Gold Mystery Series
Braddock's Gold
Hunter's Moon
Fool's Wisdom
Killing Darkness

Florida Murder Mystery Series
Death at Windover
Murder at the Canaveral Diner
Murder at the Indian River
Murder at Seminole Pond
Murder of Cowboy Gene
Murder in the Family

If I'd waited to get it perfect, I'd never done anything.
Margaret Atwood

Chapter 1

Words have no power to impress the mind without the exquisite horror of their reality. Edgar Allen Poe

If Speedy had known what waited for him that day, he'd stayed in bed. He woke with a splitting headache, not from too much alcohol, but his sinus condition. Something bloomed in the central Florida flora, and it had his number. The pain behind his eyes felt terrible, but he decided to take two Tylenol, go to work, and hope for the best. His discovery would make him forget about his headache, but still wish he'd stayed in bed.

The swamp seemed deep and like gumbo as Speedy Vanderjack probed it with the big hydraulic arm bucket of the huge backhoe. He scooped up bucket after bucket of the stinking muck and placed it to the side where he was making a connecting road. Sweat rolled down his face and chest from the extreme heat. He swatted away hungry mosquitoes that ignored the cloud from the short cigar he smoked and the 100% DEET mosquito repellent he wore. One bit at his scarred nose still healing from the removal of cancerous spots. He smacked it with his right hand. A bloody spot in his palm showed he had killed the little bloodsucker. "That'll teach you, you little beggar, not to mess with this country boy," he said out loud.

It was just another typical sweltering day in the last week of August in 1985. Speedy worked his backhoe excavator through the Florida swamp a dozen miles from Kennedy Space Center, but this would be no ordinary day for Speedy. He'd been building roads for an upscale housing development. Much of the swampy area was to be left natural, and only the higher areas in the thousand acres would be developed. The tricky part was connecting the helter-skelter high, and the dry regions locally called hammocks with roads for access through the mucky wetlands. The typical summer rains had been late

1

in coming and the year, up until two weeks ago, had been unusually hot and dry, but the skies had opened up, and the rains had come in deluges lately.

Now, with water back in the marshlands, Vanderjack had an easier time deciding where the road layout in the development would be, but the swamp, overflowing from the rains, had also produced a dangerous problem. He had to be careful with the big machine. Even with its tank-like tracks, it could still disappear into the black waters if the land under it was not firm enough to hold its weight. He was having a particularly difficult time finding solid footing between two oak and pine-covered island hammocks.

Rarely did he see anyone as he worked his way through the swampland though he often had the creepy feeling he was being watched. He sometimes spoke out loud just to hear the comforting sound of a human voice, even if it was only his own. He appreciated having a boss that trusted him completely to do the right thing. Some he remembered had been jerks watching his every move. Vanderjack had first met his present employer while clearing a lot in the front of the new development. A man pulled up in an old pickup truck and had watched him work for two hours. Curiosity had gotten the best of Speedy who turned off his land clearing machine and went over to speak with the man in the truck.

After the standard greetings and sizing up the other and his intentions, the man commented that he noted Vanderjack was very careful not to damage any trees or natural vegetation than was absolutely necessary with the bulky machine. Speedy had told him he had been instructed to do so by the lot owner and that he liked to leave things as native Florida as he could. At that point, the man identified himself as Jim Crane, owner and developer of the Windover project and offered him a job doing road and site development. He needed a conscientious man like Speedy, and so he was hired. That was two years ago, and Speedy was happy to have one construction job so long and for a man who was a great boss, but today he was using every bit of skill he had to find a place for the new road in the quagmire.

He dropped a full bucket of the watery muck on the emerging roadbed after extending the bucket as far as he could reach to a mound of peat barely sticking out of the black water and pulling it down through the swamp. Vanderjack could tell it dropped off rapidly and was deep. He would have to be careful, or he could lose his machine and possibly his life if he made the wrong move. His cigar was burned down to nothing, so he stopped, threw it in the swamp, and lite another one. He took a long drag on it and looked off toward the muck he had just pulled up. Something caught his eye. He turned off his machine, climbed down over the muddy track, and walked the short distance to the oozing pile. *What's a big, round rock doing in this Florida swamp?* He'd seen rocks similar to this in his native Michigan. Glaciers made round rocks, but there had never been any glaciers in Florida. Curious, he picked up the wet object and spun it around in his hands.

Muck flowed from three holes of the rock, but this was no ordinary rock. It was a skull, a human skull. He gasped and nearly choked as the acidic cigar fumes filled his lungs. He coughed, stepped back, slipped in the muck and almost fell.

The flesh had long since gone from it. He looked around the muck pile and found another skull of similar condition. He picked the second one up and now had two empty faces staring at him. Were there any more? Still holding the two skulls, he walked around the pile. What he saw next brought terror to his heart. A small, slightly decomposed human hand lay in the dirt. He dropped the two skulls and said something like, "Oh, sugar," only maybe stronger. Only he knows for sure.

What had he stumbled onto? He had to tell his boss and probably the local law. Someone needed to know of this. What had he found?

Chapter 2

Speedy Vanderjack burst through the door of the building that housed the office of ECS, developer of the Windover project. Janet Riggins, secretary and sales official, sat at her desk doing some paperwork. Startled by Speedy's sudden appearance and his disturbed look, she asked, "Speedy, what's wrong?"

"Where's the boss?" he said as he panted. "I have to see him *now*."

She said, "He's in his office, but he said…"

Speedy never heard the last of her sentence as he ran past her, opened the door to Mr. Crane's office and entered. He looked around but saw no one. The flush of a toilet told him the man he wanted to see so badly was in the bathroom. "Mr. Crane," he exclaimed, "I need to see you *now*."

A muffled answer came from the bathroom. "Be right there in a minute."

Speedy waited impatiently and paced around. Mr. Crane came out of the bathroom and said, "Now, what the Sam Hill is so important a man can't even be left alone when he's on the porcelain throne?"

"Boss, you ain't never gonna believe this. I was out working at the end of the road at that place where we knew we were gonna have trouble finding a way for the road through the marsh," Speedy said, but he was interrupted by Mr. Crane.

"Yes, I know the place you are referring to, but what's got you so in such a tizzy?"

"Real trouble, boss, and not the road construction type."

"Well, what is it then?" Mr. Crane said.

4

Speedy continued, "I was out there diggin' around feeling the marsh banks and swamp bottoms with my big excavator backhoe for a good place for the road. I dug up and dumped about ten buckets of muck when something in a pile caught my eye. I got off my big machine and walked over to the pile. What I thought was two round rocks was two human skulls. They looked to me like they had been in the ground a long time."

Mr. Crane exclaimed, "Two skulls? No wonder you're excited."

Vanderjack cut in, "But boss, that's not the worst of it. I walked around the pile and found a human hand that still had flesh on it."

Mr. Crane's eyes grew wide. "Good Lord," he said. "We need to call the police on this." He turned around and saw Janet standing in the doorway. "Did you hear all this?" he asked.

"Yes, I did," she said. "I'll give the boys in blue a call and tell them what Speedy found."

"You do that," Mr. Crane replied. "I think I need to see this before the cops do." He turned to Speedy. "Speedy, we'll take your truck back, and you show me where and what you found."

"Boss," he said. "We better take your old Jeep and not your car. I was in such a big hurry and so frightened, I went right past my truck and ran all the way here. Even with the muddy road hindering me, I know I made the mile here in under four minutes."

Mr. Crane realized the truth in what Speedy said. He nodded, grabbed the keys to the Jeep off the nail on the wall, and said, "Let's go."

The trio left Mr. Crane's office. Janet went to her desk and grabbed the phone. She yelled to the two men as they neared the exit door. "Mr. Crane, do you have the walkie-talkie so I can contact you when I get the police on the way?"

The two men stopped and looked sheepishly at each other. "No," answered Mr. Crane, who walked to her desk and took the one Janet had in her hand.

"Thanks. Don't know what I would do without you," he said and quickly left the building with Speedy in tow.

The door slammed shut, and Janet said to herself. "I know what you would do. You'd forget your head if it wasn't attached."

Then, she smiled. "Guess I have job security as long as he remains absent-minded, and I don't see that point changing, Mr. Crane." She shook her head and began dialing the rotary phone.

Outside, the two men walked rapidly to the Jeep. They pulled off the tarp which covered the Jeep, threw the tarp on a woodpile, and climbed in. A cat ran from under the seat and frightened the jittery men who screamed like little girls. They looked at each other with embarrassment. "I'm not saying nothin' about this," said Mr. Crane.

Speedy looked at his boss. "Me neither. It didn't happen. There was no cat here, and we didn't scream like girls."

"Right," said Mr. Crane. "No cat, no scream, nothin' happened."

They got in the old topless Jeep. A roll bar and a winch in front were the only additions to the vehicle. Mr. Crane had bought it unassembled from Army surplus and built it himself. He turned the key in the ignition switch, and the starter growled as did the engine. Mr. Crane pumped the gas and pulled the choke. "Come on, Nellie Belle, you can do it. Come on, girl. We need to go."

Speedy looked at Mr. Crane. "Nellie Belle? You named her Nellie Belle?"

"Yeah, I always like the Roy Rogers show. You got a problem with Nellie Belle?"

Speedy Vanderjack was no dummy. He smiled. "No, boss, no."

Mr. Crane pumped the gas pedal two more times, and Speedy said eagerly, "Come on, Nellie Belle. Come on, girl."

Whether it was Speedy's encouraging words or the extra gas in the carburetor, they would never know, but the old Jeep roared to life. Mr. Crane smiled with satisfaction, put the manual transmission in first gear, and let out the clutch. They were off down the muddy, potholed road to where Speedy had been working. It only took a few minutes to reach that site. Mr. Crane stopped the Jeep, and the two men got out. They walked past the big bucket excavator to the muck pile.

"There's the two skulls I told you about," said Speedy, who now walked to the other side of the muck pile, "and here's the hand."

Mr. Crane studied the two skulls. "Yeah, I can see why you thought they were ancient. They sure look it." He paused. "Now, where's that decomposing hand?"

"Right here," Speedy said. He moved closer and pointed.

"Don't touch it," Mr. Crane warned. "That could well be evidence of a crime."

"I won't. I'm thinkin' like you are. I've watched enough of those cop detective shows to know not to mess up what could be a murder scene."

Mr. Crane nodded his head and said, "You were right in reporting this. I don't like the looks of this at all."

Static came over the walkie-talkie followed by Janet's voice. "Mr. Crane, I have news."

"Okay Janet, what've you got?" he asked into the wireless device.

"I tried the FHP barracks of the state police down the road, but they said they only did wrecks and traffic control, you know, speeding tickets, DWIs and similar. Next, I called the Brevard County Sheriff's Department. They said from my description of the location; they weren't sure if it was their jurisdiction or the town of Canaveral Flats. Either way, the two departments work together, and an officer from each will be there ASAP. Could be an hour wait, though."

Mr. Crane whistled through his teeth and shook his head. He looked at Speedy and said, "Speedy, why don't you take the rest of the day off? You look like you need some time to recover from this scare. Stop in the office tomorrow morning at the usual time. We'll see if the cops will let us work here or we could go over to the south 40 and work there. Either way, we're done for the day here."

Speedy sighed. "That's good with me. My stomach's in an uproar, and this spot is no place to make a mistake with my big machine. I've seen machines this big and bigger disappear in the peat bogs of Michigan when the operator made a careless mistake. You need total concentration when working in a place like this. One of my union brothers drowned when he made a misstep and went down with his machine. I can still see his wife and two teenage daughters crying at the funeral." He sighed again. "I think it was finally real to them their husband, and daddy wasn't coming home again."

"I'm no expert on this matter, but from the look at that hand, someone did not come home recently either. I'll stay here until the cops come. If they need to talk to you, they can reach you at your home."

Speedy was about to say something when he heard a faint siren. The two men looked down the muddy road. A Chevy truck with two men inside was coming quickly. Blue lights flashed from the light bar on top of the vehicle.

Mr. Crane said, "Looks like the cops got here sooner than expected. You better stay and tell them what and how you found the remains."

Speedy nodded and said, "Looks like I may be late for supper. I have a feeling this could take a while."

"I think you're right," said Mr. Crane. "I think you are right."

Chapter 3

The big Chevy truck with the flashing blue lights rolled to a stop ten feet from the two men. A man in a green uniform with a patch on the shoulder that read, "Brevard County Deputy," got out of the truck on the driver's side and a tall, lanky man in a white shirt with short sleeves and dark blue trousers exited the other side. Both were armed, the former with a 15 shot 9 mm pistol and the latter with a large caliber revolver. "Hello, Mr. Crane. Your secretary said we could find you here."

Mr. Crane squinted his eyes from the sun and said, "Why, Deputy DeWitt, I haven't seen you in a month of Sundays. How's the wife and the twins?"

"Finer than frog hair split three ways. The twins are taller than me now, but skinny as rails. Both of them together soppin' wet don't weigh what I do." He tugged at his ample belly. "My wife's cookin' is famous all around these parts, as you well know. And this is Chief of Police Bill Kenney. We were doin' a joint training operation nearby when we got the call and came right over."

Officer Kenney stuck his hand out toward Mr. Crane, who met it. "Pleased to meet you, Mr. Crane. People had been talking about your development and how you were taking extra care not to disturb the environment any more than absolutely necessary."

"And I'm pleased to meet you, too." The two men released hands, and Mr. Crane said, "Glad people are noticin' our work, and this here is Speedy Vanderjack. He made the discovery you are here about."

The Chief of Police and Speedy shook hands. Then, Speedy shook hands with the deputy. "Now that everyone knows everyone, Speedy, could you tell us what happened?"

"Sure," he said. "I was using my big backhoe machine," and he pointed to it, "to try to find a place for a roadway through this mucky swamp. I made several scoops from over here to that little black peaty spot," and he pointed again, "made this pile we're standin' by when something unusual in it caught my eye. At first, I thought it was some rocks, but they turned out to be skulls, and then I found a decaying hand on the other side of the pile. Liked to freaked me out and I ran to the office and told Mr. Crane. Janet, our secretary, called the police. Mr. Crane wanted to see it, so we took his Jeep here and then you guys showed up."

"Did you move any of the evidence?" asked Deputy DeWitt.

"I didn't know what the skulls were until I picked up the first. I couldn't believe what I found until I picked up the second. I walked around the backside, and that's where I found the hand. I was scared to death, and I dropped the skulls and ran all the way to the office."

The men walked to the backside of the pile and examined the remains. "What do you think?" said Mr. Crane to the two lawmen.

The two men looked at the remains and the area thoughtfully. It was a full minute before Officer Kenney spoke, "I'm no expert on this, but the skulls look old. The hand belonged to a young boy or maybe a young woman and was buried fairly recently. I'd bet a dollar to a donut, the rest of what we're looking for is in the area Speedy disturbed with his big machine."

The deputy nodded his head in agreement. "That would be my guess, too. We need to get the coroner out to gather up the remains, especially the hand before it decomposes any more or critters try to eat it. Between the fire ants, possums, and coyotes, nothing lasts long out in a place like this."

"And don't forget the heat," said Officer Kenney.

"Okay, I'll call for the coroner on the radio, and you take some pictures with that newfangled 35 mm camera of yours," replied the deputy.

"Will do," he said.

"Anything we can do?" asked Mr. Crane.

"Could you give me a few minutes to answer that question?" said Officer Kenney. "I need to get some pictures before the coroner arrives and I'm working some ideas in my head on that."

"Okay," said Mr. Crane. "I can wait a few minutes, but we need to get back to work."

Officer Kenney nodded that he had heard and understood the other man. He continued to take lots of pictures and stopped to reload twice.

The deputy returned and said, "Well, I have good news and bad news for you, Bill. The coroner is on the way. That's the good news."

"So what's the bad news?" asked Officer Bill Kenney.

"I gave headquarters a detailed description of our location," answered Deputy DeWitt, "and they tell me this little spot of land we're on is in that crazy dogleg part of your jurisdiction, Canaveral Flats. They told me you can expect minimal help from the county."

"What?" exclaimed Officer Kenney. "The town has an agreement with the county for help on matters like this. I've only had basic training on processing a possible crime scene. What reason did they give?"

"Seems the county hired some new bean counter accountant fresh out of college, and he saw how much Canaveral Flats was in arrears for work the sheriff's department had done for the town. There won't be any more help until the debt's brought up-to-date."

Officer Kenney stood with a shocked look on his face. He looked at the deputy and said, "I can't believe they'd do this. The town is slow in paying, but the bill always gets paid. You got to help me. Is there nothing you can do? Where am I going to find someone to process a complex investigation like this? It has all the markings of a crime scene in Indian burial grounds, or maybe even a dumping ground for a mass execution. Who am I gonna find with qualifications for this? Our town's always stretched for money."

"I don't know," answered the deputy, "but don't expect any help from the county until that new bean counter comes to his senses or gets the riot act read to him by the county commissioners, and I would not hold my breath if I were you. Sorry, Bill, but I think you're gonna have to solve this problem on your own."

Officer Bill Kenney shook his head. What was he going to do? He walked over to where the hand was lying. Somewhere someone knew who the hand belonged to and they were missing this person. He believed a serious crime had been committed, and someone needed to be brought to face justice, but how could he do it all by himself?

"Officer Kenney," said Mr. Crane, "could I make a suggestion?"

"Sure," he answered, "what d'ya got?"

"I don't know much about police work, but I do know a lot about developing property. We start with a plan and go from there," said Mr. Crane.

"Please, go on," said Officer Kenney.

"I've always been a curious guy, too curious some people tell me, but I would like to see justice done too, and I'm also interested in those old skulls. Who knows what else is in that swamp?"

"What did you have in mind, Mr. Crane?" asked the officer.

"You need to get in that swamp to process whatever we have here," said Mr. Crane. "You need to have that area separated from the rest of the marsh and dewatered." He turned to Speedy and asked, "Speedy, how long would it take you to do that?"

Speedy looked at his boss and could tell he was serious on this plan. He looked at the swamp and let out a little whistle. "It would take me the rest of the day to get the well points and pumps from storage, then about half-day to make some berms, and the rest of the day to place the well points in the berms. It should all be pumped out overnight if it doesn't rain and you know what the weather is like this time of year, afternoon deluges and tropical disturbances."

"Okay," said Mr. Crane, "I want it done ASAP." Speedy nodded that he understood. Mr. Crane said to the officer, "I've got you started. Now, you need to find someone qualified to oversee this investigation."

"Yeah," said the small-town lawman, "and one who will work for little or nothing." He mused for a moment. "And I think I know where to start, but there's this one little problem."

Chapter 4

The county coroner, a competent man named Will Corbett, had arrived in a four-wheel-drive van about an hour after the deputy, Mr. Crane, and Speedy Vanderjack had left. Bill Kenney had spent the time looking around the area and trying to come up with a possible scenario on how the decomposing hand had ended up in what seemed to be an ancient burial site. It was most likely that the hand was attached to a body, as yet undiscovered, that's still buried in the peat. The summer had been very dry, one of the worst droughts Bill Kenney had seen in the twenty years since he left the hills of West Virginia. Up until the recent rains, the road leading to this site would have been high and dry. A man or woman driving any two-wheel-drive car could have easily made it to the site and buried a body or part of a body then.

He pondered if this could be the murder site or whether it was elsewhere. It was too soon to tell. The coroner had asked if he was done processing the hand. He was, and the coroner collected the hand and the skulls. He made some preliminary observations which he said could change once he took a closer look in the lab. Yes, he believed the hand was recent, and the skulls looked old, very old. It was probably a crime scene in the newly discovered, yet ancient burial ground, which was actually a burial pond. There were several other burial ponds in the state of Florida, and these were found nowhere else on earth. Yes, he felt there was more of the body in the peat and Bill should call the coroner immediately if and when he found it. Will Corbett put the hand on ice in a cooler he had brought, and each skull went into a five-gallon plastic bucket. He gave a third bucket to the officer and told him it would make a handy place to sit.

Bill turned it upside down and sat on it. He laughed to himself as he remembered an old pipefitter he knew. Mr. Boggs had said when he died that the mortician would find the words Five Gallon pressed forever on his behind as he had spent so much time at work sitting on an upturned five-gallon bucket. The coroner said he would let Officer Kenney know when he had news on any of the remains and added that Bill could call him at the county office whenever he needed. Bill Kenney thanked the coroner for his professional interest to which Will Corbett replied, "I almost hate my job. I'm tired of looking at dead bodies, especially the children and murder victims. Both died too soon. I keep doing my work because I want justice and closure for all who have lost their loved ones and if I can bring this to them, I will, if at all possible, as long as I'm the coroner."

Will. Corbett said little more, took the buckets and cooler to the van and got in. It only took a moment before he was out of sight. Bill Kenney sat in the silence and listened to the wind blow through the Spanish moss-covered oak tree that sheltered him. A few birds chirped and called to one another and then grew silent. He heard what he thought was a frog jumping into the water, but he remained unsure about what had made the noise. A creepy feeling came over him. Was he being watched by someone hidden in the swamp, or had the spirits of the dead been awakened, and they were none too happy to have their sleep disturbed?

The noise of an engine broke the eerie silence and then he saw Speedy Vanderjack's backhoe pulling a trailer loaded with long plastic pipes of various sizes. Bill recognized these as components for the dewatering. After pulling the trailer as far off of the road as possible, Speedy disconnected it from the backhoe and drove the big machine over to Bill. The two men discussed how big and where the four sides of the temporary pond would be. After some give and take, they agreed, and Speedy began under the watchful eye of the lawman. He worked without stopping until the sun was on the western horizon. At that point, he pulled the backhoe over to Officer Bill and said, "Unless you have an invisible car somewhere out here in the swamp, I'd advise you to get on the backhoe for a ride back to civilization."

"I was hoping to hear that offer an hour or so ago," said Bill.

They rode the bouncing machine down the muddy road to the main office without speaking. Both were tired. As they neared the building, Speedy slowed the machine down at a large hump in the road. Bill saw his opportunity and asked, "Do you ever close off this road?"

"No," said Speedy. "Never saw any need to."

"Well," Bill Kenney replied, "I think we have reason to now."

Speedy turned his head to the lawman and nodded. After they went a little farther to a place where the road had deep canals on each side, Speedy turned the backhoe sideways and fully extended the rear bucket and then front scoop out as far as they could go, completely blocking the road. Not even a motorcycle could get through the barricade. "I believe this will do."

Officer Bill Kenney responded, "I agree. It'll be good to get out of here, but I still have something I need to do tonight or early tomorrow - find me someone qualified to oversee this operation."

"You have someone in mind?"

"Yeah, but there's a problem. Spirits."

"Spirits?" Speedy said. "What is this guy, a shaman, or a witch doctor or something like that?"

"Those would be easy to deal with. The most qualified man I know is a drunk that hasn't been sober once in the last year," said Bill Kenney.

"You've got to be kidding," said Speedy.

"Wish I was, but my list of candidates has only one name on it."

"Good luck. You're gonna need it."

"Yup," said Officer Bill Kenney, and then he sighed, "I'm sure gonna need it."

Chapter 5

It was another hot and muggy morning in Central Florida when Officer Bill Kenney drove his personal pickup down the washboard sandy roads that made up Canaveral Flats. The town roads were set up like a checkerboard grid, but there was only one real road connecting the little town of three hundred to the outside world. The other way out was known only by a few, and they rarely used it. On this main connecting road sat the only store serving the people of Canaveral Flats. Anything from beer to bread to laxatives could be purchased at Miller's General Store. They had all kinds of products for whether you needed incoming or outgoing. It also had the town post office inside, so there was a lot of foot traffic into the old wooden building that desperately needed a new coat of paint.

As usual, Fred Miller, an autistic young man, sat on a bench on the front porch. He helped in the store with his elderly mother. Fred sat on that porch every day and watched the people come and go. He never looked people in the eye, and always spoke of himself in the third person. No one paid much attention to Fred as they came and went. If Fred did look in your direction, which was not often, it seemed he was looking right through you at something in the distance behind you, but Fred saw, and he remembered.

Chief Bill Kenney parked his pickup in front of the store and walked up the steps. "Sorry, the store's closed today till ten o'clock. Momma had to go to Cocoa on business," Fred said, who did not turn his head to speak to Bill Kenney.

"Well, thanks, Fred, but I need to get this mail out ASAP," Bill Kenney replied.

Fred continued to look straight ahead and said, "We can take it for you. We can give it to Momma when she returns."

Bill Kenney said to Fred, "Fred, can I trust you to see this mail goes right in when your Momma gets back? It's really important."

Fred's expression did not change. "We are trustworthy and honest. Momma always told us to be honest all the time, even if sometimes the truth wasn't something some people wanted to hear."

"That sounds like your Momma, and her approval is good enough for me." He handed the letters to Fred. "Now, you take good care of them for me."

Fred continued to look forward and said, "We will see nothin' happens to your mail."

Bill Kenney turned and began walking down the steps. He heard Fred's voice say, "Later, gator."

Bill stopped and turned back toward Fred. "After a while, crocodile."

Fred turned toward Bill Kenney, but as usual, he seemed to be looking right through the man in front of him. Fred raised his right hand and held it Indian style. "Go in peace," he said.

"Thank you, Fred. You do the same." Fred continued to stare off into the distance.

Bill Kenney got into his pickup and did a quick U-turn back to the little hamlet. "Peace," he said to himself. "I hope there is some for a change." *Nothing like starting the day off with a challenge.* He knew what he needed to do and hoped he could find the right words in what could be an awkward encounter.

He passed old trailers, a few ranch-style homes in decent condition, and a number of shacks that looked like a good windstorm could blow them over. Canaveral Flats was like few places on earth. The original owner of this large tract of land had cut it up in one to five-acre lots. He wanted a place that would welcome anyone, especially those the upper crust looked down on. Bill chuckled to himself as he remembered something the developer, now deceased, had said. "Why, the upper crust ain't nothin' but a bunch of crumbs held together with some dough." From Bill's observation of life, people were pretty much the same, but he had run into those that fit the old man's description.

There was no zoning, and any kind of home construction was allowed. It looked a lot like Little Abner's Dogpatch, but that was okay with Bill. This was home, and he had taken an oath to uphold the laws of the state of Florida. He did the best he could. Bill figured the meeting could go one of two ways and he hoped it did not go south. He would find out soon enough.

He pulled the truck up to the gate that barred his entry. It was locked with a cheap lock. He hopped the gate and headed to the old, rundown trailer that sat one hundred feet back on the lot. The yard didn't look like it'd been mowed in months. Dog fennel and other weeds were rapidly taking over the yard along with Brazilian Pepper bushes now getting close to small tree size.

He walked up to the screened-in porch attached to the old trailer. It looked like it had been repaired recently. Bill had been expecting a large barking dog to announce his arrival, but the dog was not to be seen anywhere. Still, he remained alert.

Knocking on the aluminum screen door did not get the attention of the owner. He opened the door and walked in. There to the left sleeping in an overstuffed chair which had seen better days, was his quarry, Roger Pyles. A half-empty Wild Turkey bourbon bottle sat between his legs. A thirty-gallon trash can with a split at the base and filled to overflowing with liquor bottles, and beer cans sat next to the sleeping man.

"Good morning," said Chief of Police Kenney to the sleeping man who continued to snore. He said, "Good morning," again, but still had no response. Bill Kenney was a patient man, but drunks, especially those he knew, could try his patience.

"Good morning," he shouted at the sleeping man.

Roger Pyles' body jerked on the La-Z-Boy chair. He turned his head to where the disturbing noise had come from. His hair was long, uncombed, and fell in his face. Saliva trailed from his mouth down his beard. It appeared to Bill Kenney that the man had not bathed or changed his clothes in a month. Through hangover glazed eyes, Roger looked at Bill. "Bill," he said, "what are you doing here? You got a lot of gall sneaking up on a man like that. Why didn't the dog bark at you like he does at everyone else?"

"That's a good question," said Bill. "Where's your big dog?"

It took a few seconds for the wretch to respond. "Oh, now I remember. He died a month ago. Got to get another one, so people don't walk away with the place and disturb my sleep."

"Roger, you look like hell. You can't keep this up. Liquor is going to kill you sooner or later."

Roger's head wobbled as he spoke, "Well, it's my life to waste, ain't it? If I want to drink myself to death, I will."

Bill asked, "If you want to die, why don't you shoot yourself and get it over with? I know you got a gun."

Roger looked Bill in the eye and said, "That would be too fast, and I ain't done punishing myself yet. And I like to drink. You ain't gonna stop me."

"Roger," said Bill. "I'm not here today as the friend you've known for years. I'm here as a law officer with two choices. What I do depends on you. Number one, you can help me as only you can with a case that's been dropped in my lap, or…."

Roger interrupted, **"Or what?"**

Chief Bill Kenney gritted his teeth. "Or under the authority invested in me by the State of Florida for situations like this, I'm taking you to the hospital so you can dry out."

"What?" cried Roger as his lanky, 6-foot 2-inch body unsteadily rose to his feet. For a split second, Bill remembered why Roger was sometimes mistaken for Sam Elliott, the movie star. They looked and sounded similar.

"You heard me," answered Chief Kenney with all the calmness he could muster. "You'll help me or go to a drunk tank to dry out." He pulled a blackjack from his hip pocket.

Roger looked at the smaller man with the weapon in his hand. "Hey, those things are illegal. You could hurt someone badly with one of those."

Firmly, Chief Kenney said, "It's your choice."

Roger said nothing for a few seconds, and then he sat down in the old chair. "I ain't never been put in a drunk tank and don't want the personal humiliation. Just what is it you need me for, that only I can do?"

Chief Bill Kenney began, "Yesterday, not far from here inside the town limits of Canaveral Flats, human remains were found. The county won't help, and I need someone with experience both in crime scene analysis and archaeological recovery of human remains. I think a young woman was murdered and buried in an ancient burial pond. There's several of them we know of in the state. A backhoe operator dug up a slightly decomposed human hand and two skulls that look ancient. The coroner has them now. This thing is bigger than I can handle. I remembered reading in the paper about how you helped solve several cases for the police when you lived up north. And you were a professor, a Ph.D., doctor of some kind of archaeology, and knew bunches on digs in ancient cultural sites. I'd don't know who else has the background for this, but you."

Roger Pyles stroked his scruffy beard with his hand. His friend from childhood knew a lot about him, but not everything, or he was conveniently leaving details out. He thought for a moment. He wasn't going to a drunk tank and now that his quick temper was spent, Roger had no desire to fight his friend and a lawman, especially one who knew how to use a blackjack.

Roger looked at his friend's pleading face. Maybe, he, Roger, needed a change. Getting drunk every day still had its appeal, but...

"Okay, but under a few conditions," said Roger.

"You're in no position to ask for conditions."

Roger ignored the lawman's response. "Number one. No taking me to the drunk tank."

Bill Kenney responded, "Okay, as long as you are sober enough to help me."

"Fair enough," said Roger Pyles, "and you just answered my second question. I can drink as long as I'm sober on the job."

"That is correct," replied Bill. "I need you now, and going cold turkey could produce the DTs, and we don't want that."

"Number three. I think I'll take a bath and get my hair cut. Know a good barber?"

"Yeah, just go over to US 1. Look for Larry's. It's where I get mine cut and if Larry's not there, ask for Linda. She's probably better than the boss and good looking, too."

Roger asked, "Well-built is she?"

"And pleasant to look at while she cuts your hair."

"I think I get the picture and one more request." He paused. "Where's the county dog pound? I need a big dog to keep the riff-raff off my property?"

Bill Kenney thought he saw a hint of a smile on the gnarly face. How he hoped his friend had not gone down the drunkard highway too far to ever to return. "Tell you what. You do what you said you needed to do today, and tomorrow, I'll take you by the crime/archaeological site so you can have a look-see, and we'll go by the pound afterward."

Roger replied, "Sounds like a plan. I'll see you in the morning."

Chief Kenney opened the screen door, walked toward the gate, hopped over it, and then climbed in the old vehicle. It soon disappeared down Canaveral Flats Boulevard.

Roger sat in the grungy chair and thought. *If I'm gonna do this, I need a shower. Wonder if the water heater still works? I haven't turned it on in a while.*

He looked at the bottle of bourbon next to him, picked it up, and took a big swig. He set the bottle back down and got up. *I better get that shower. Don't want to go to no drunk tank, but what did I agree to? Maybe the drunk tank wasn't such a bad option, but Bill needs me, and you don't let friends down. Guess I better do what I said I would and see him in the morning. Wonder what I got myself into?*

Chapter 6

Canaveral Flats Chief of Police Bill Kenney wheeled his pickup truck down the washboard sandy streets of the town. *Someone had a real sense of humor when he named this potholed street Canaveral Flats Boulevard.*

He passed Miller's General Store and saw Fred sitting on the bench in front. Chief Kenney waved at Fred, and as usual, Fred ignored him, but he knew Fred saw him and would remember. Soon he arrived at the old trailer Roger Pyles called home and parked his truck in front. Bill opened the gate and walked to the trailer. He noted the pickup truck that sat in the yard had been moved since he was there yesterday. Snoring greeted him at the screened-in porch. Chief Kenney studied the man sleeping in the La-Z-Boy chair. Roger had a new haircut, his beard was trimmed, he looked clean in the new clothes he wore, but he appeared drunk just like yesterday.

"Roger," he said, but Roger continued to snore. "Roger," he said a little louder, but the snoring continued.

Guess I should be happy with the improvement, and not ride him so hard. He's been through a world of hurtin'.

Chief Kenney opened the screen door and walked in. He stopped next to the snoring man, pulled out his billy club, hit the side of the shoe of the sleeping man, and backed away. Surprised drunks were unpredictable, and one needed to be prepared for whatever. Roger Pyles opened one eye and looked at Bill Kenney. "You just ruined a great dream, flat foot," he said.

Bill Kenney laughed, "And what was it about, Sleeping Beauty?"

Roger Pyles looked puzzled. "Can't remember, but it was a doozie, and you ruined it." He stretched in the chair and looked at Bill Kenney. "I got to get me a dog."

"Yeah, I know. You never know what kind of riff-raff will show up," Officer Kenney said.

"Exactly," Roger replied. "You still need my help? I cleaned up my act just for you."

Bill Kenney grimaced, "Yeah, the outside looks better, but I think you're still drunk."

"You said I didn't need to quit, just slow down, so I only drank half a fifth instead of the whole thing," dragging out the last two words.

Bill Kenney shook his head. After dealing with many drunks over the years, he was surprised to see as much change as he did in the man before him, but he was not going to admit that to him. "You're drunk," he replied.

"No, I ain't. I know what drunk is, and this is just feelin' no pain."

Officer Bill Kenney could see there was no point in arguing. "Did you get your hair cut over at Larry's?"

"Yup, Linda did it. Larry was working on a head, and she wasn't, so I had her do it. She is a looker. Got a big front porch, too."

"I hope you didn't stare at it too much," Officer Kenney said.

"Well, I did try to be discrete about it. I ain't a complete doofus, you know," Roger replied.

"Good thing for you. I forgot to tell you that big knuckle dragger Larry is her husband, and he don't take kindly to men staring at her."

"Now, you tell me."

"Sorry about that. When I first started going there, they didn't know me from Adam's house cat. Larry and Linda were both busy. Larry had just got done shaving a man with a straight razor, and I noticed that he noticed how the guy in Linda's chair was staring at her. Like any good cop does, I was aware of what was going on. I could see Larry getting madder and madder. His neck was turning red, and when he could take it no more, he yelled at the man in her chair, 'Quite starin' at her boobies if you know what's good for you' The fellow's eyes got the size of saucers when he looked at big Larry and the straight razor in his hand. He let out a cry that would wake the dead, jumped up out of the chair, and ran out the door with the barber's cape still around him and Larry in hot pursuit.

Larry stopped at the door and yelled something I would rather not repeat at the fleeing man. When he came back in, he said, 'Don't like men staring at my wife.' He still had the straight razor in his hand, so I nodded in agreement. The man, who Larry had just given a shave to, looked scared. Larry picked up on that, grunted, 'Your lucky day. It's on the house.' Larry went in the backroom to cool off, shut the door behind him, and the man exited quickly via the front door. Linda pointed for me to sit in her chair. I wondered if I should run for the door too, but decided to take the chair. Linda got me all prepped for my haircut and started to work."

He continued, "I didn't say anything and tried not to look. She put me at ease when she spoke to me. I never will forget what she said." He stopped.

"What'd she say? What'd she say?" asked Roger.

"She said, 'Pay no attention to my husband. He's more bark than bite. He loves me, big boobs and all, and actually, I like the way it makes him jealous. Shows he cares.' I nodded in agreement. She continued, 'He don't really mind if you look a little. I mean, when I'm in front of you working, where else are you gonna look? Just don't stare, okay?' I was surprised at how candid she was, but I guess she felt I needed an explanation about what had just happened. I nodded in agreement again.

She went on, 'Had a fellow in here a while back. Never been here before, but I knew he was the head deacon at the local Baptist church. When I was in front of him workin', what a mess that was. He turned his head right then left, trying not to look. I thought I was goin' to cut one of his ears off the way he was jerkin' around trying not to look. Finally, I was frustrated and told him to shut his eyes if it would help. He did, and I worked on a steady head of hair. He kept his eyes shut for another five minutes even after I'd done the front and now working on the sides and back. Guess he was prayin' for forgiveness.' She laughed as did I."

Bill continued, "Then she said, 'Yeah, to us, you're just another head of hair. To an ice cream vendor, you're just another dip, and to a doctor giving a colonoscopy, you're just another…, you know,' and we both laughed again."

"I said to her, 'You can put people at ease. You're a natural.' She said, 'Yeah, you develop the gift of gab working with the public.' I nodded in agreement. She said, 'Pay no attention to Larry. My husband is a great guy. Been in a little trouble, but that's in the past.'"

"I said to her, 'Lots of people move down here for a new start.' She said, 'I got in some trouble back in Morgantown, West Virginia, too, and met him on a community service thingie. We hit it off, and I moved in with him. He put me through barber school, we got married, and here we are today.' Then I said, 'Go Mountaineers. I'm from over in Mineral County around between Keyser and just south of Cumberland, Maryland, across the Potomac.' She said, 'Yeah, still love the Mountaineers, but we also root for the Florida teams now. I'm a Florida State Seminoles fan, but he likes the University of Florida Gators. We're a house divided.'"

"I laughed at that. A lot of folks in Florida have that problem. Then she said, 'We have some fun with it. When they play, we have a standing bet. If I win, he has to do what I say and call me His Ladyship or My Queen and do whatever I ask, within reason, and if he wins, I must call him His Lordship or My King and do whatever he asks, within reason, of course.'"

"I replied, 'Within reason, of course. I understand completely. Paybacks are hell.' She smiled coyly, nodded her head and spoke, 'We went to the last Gator-Seminole game in Gainesville, and the Seminoles won, so he had to treat me like royalty all the rest of the day, opening the door, bowing to me, even at the restaurant we stopped at in Ocala on the way back here. I think he's actually a better sport about it than I would be, but we'll see if and when the Gators ever beat the Seminoles.' I chuckled at that, and she went on, 'Even as tired as we were, I treated him royally in the sack, if you get my drift.'"

"I nodded and added, 'Once a king, always a king…' And she completed it, 'But once a night's enough.' We both laughed, and she snickered, 'My old king said he was up for more than once and he was.' I was a little surprised. She read my face and said, 'I enjoyed it too. He was still sleeping the next morning, so I made him a king-size breakfast, served it to him in bed, and then we wasted the morning away wrapped in each other's arms.' I commented that it was time well wasted. She nodded 'yes' and, to move things along, after all, I still needed her to finish my hair and not talk so much, I added, 'I bet you hear all kinds of things from people while you are working on their hair.'"

"She nodded in agreement and then asked me what I did for a living. I smiled and told her I was the town cop for Canaveral Flats. Her eyes got big, and she took in a sharp, quick breath, so I smiled even more and told her not to worry about what I'd seen. All's well that ends well, and I saw no reason to mention it no more. She sighed, relieved, and then proceeded to complete one of the best haircuts I'd ever had. Between you and me, I think she's better than Larry, especially with people with the wavy hair like I have, and she's got on her pretty little noggin also. Gave her a nice tip, too, I did. Great people, just don't stare."

"Wish you had told me this sooner," Roger said, and he gave a sigh of relief. "Looks like I passed the test and came out unharmed."

"Larry's really a good guy and sure cares about his wife. He's very protective, and that's one of the things she admires about him," Chief Bill said.

"You learned all that in one sitting?"

"Most of it. Not the first time I had been in there. As I said, cops are observant. You see them in a public setting like a restaurant, and besides sitting with their backs to a wall, their eyes are always moving to look at each person who enters to see if they are a threat or not. You're trained to be observant in your line of work, too."

"Okay, gotcha. Tell me what else is new since I last saw you?" Roger asked.

The chief began, "I called Mr. Crane at Windover this morning. He reported the site I want you to investigate has been dewatered but was moist, mucky, and slippery. I have some tools for you to use: boots, latex gloves, a shovel, spade, paintbrush, toothbrush, and a gallon sprayer, and oh yeah, a camera. I want lots of pictures for the records. And make lots of notes in the spiral notebook I'm giving you, okay?"

26

"Okay, okay," Roger answered. "I get the picture. Whatever I find may be evidence of a crime scene. I've done this before. It's not my first rodeo, you know? And by the way, I don't do latex. Found out I was allergic to the stuff in the bad old days, when I was a horny young stud that chases the fillies, used a latex condom, and broke out in a terrible rash on my favorite organ. Never made that mistake again."

"More information than I needed to know," Bill Kenney said. He had a silly smile on face as he thought about what Roger had just said. "I'll see you get non-latex gloves before you start work at the burial site."

Half drunk or not, Chief Bill Kenney knew his best hope of getting to the bottom of what had happened at the Windover Pond was the man still reclining in the overstuffed chair before him. "Good, now get outta that chair, stand up straight and raise your right hand."

Roger Pyles did as he was told. "Okay, now what?"

"By the authority vested in me by the State of Florida, I now make you an acting officer of the law in Canaveral Flats. Do you swear to uphold the laws of the State of Florida and act in a matter worthy of this office?"

"Whatever," Roger Pyles said. He could see the answer did not completely please the Chief of Police, so he added, "Yeah, I do."

"Good," the chief said. "You are now an officer in the Canaveral Flats Police Department."

"What's it pay?" Roger Pyles asked.

"You get one 'Get out of the Drunk Tank for Free Card' when you complete the project."

"Coming from you, Bill, it's better than I expected," and he gave a thin smile.

"Okay, let's get to work. You're coming with me. No driving in the shape you're in."

Roger smiled a little wider. "Well, what are we waiting for?"

They walked out to Chief Kenney's truck and got in. "Oh, one more thing," Roger Pyles said.

"And what's that?"

Roger replied, "After we're done today, you're taking me to the dog pound."

"Sure," laughed the officer. "They'll think you are just another of the strays I'm bringing in."

"Ain't funny," Roger growled. "Remember, you're talking to an officer of the law."

"Good point, and don't forget you're talking to your boss."

Roger snickered and said, "Aye, aye, captain."

Chief Kenney smiled. *Maybe this will work out.* He looked at the man next to him. "We'll get you a dog, a big one to protect you from the riff-raff."

"That's right. Don't know how much you need a dog until he's gone." Roger Pyles nodded his head and said, "Now let's get out to the site and see what I can find to solve this puzzle."

"Good, you never know where the evidence will lead you. If anyone can get us answers, I believe it's you."

Roger looked somewhat surprised. "Thank you for that vote of confidence. Don't think anyone else would have said I was worth wasting a bullet on. I'll try not to disappoint you."

"I'm counting on you," Chief Kenney said. He had no other options. "Let's get over there and get you to work." A thought came to the policeman. "Say, we need rubber gloves and the hardware store is over by the dog pound. We'll get the gloves and then stop at the pound and get you a dog, but we don't have all day. How does that sound?"

"Great," Roger said. "What's keeping us?"

The men hopped into Chief Kenney's pickup and headed toward Titusville. It didn't take long to get to the hardware store for gloves. Roger suggested getting some rabbit wire which he could use to sift the earth he dug up. Bill Kenney paid for both items. They left the hardware store and headed for the dog pound. It was only a short distance to it. They parked under a large oak tree. The yelping of many dogs could be heard coming from the building. They walked in and were greeted by a young woman wearing a Brevard County shirt with the name Sharon on it.

"Hello," she said. "Can I help? Looking for a dog or cat or maybe a bird or a rabbit? We have lots of animals who would love to be adopted."

"I'm looking for a dog, but I like to try one out to make sure it's the right one. Is that okay?" Roger asked.

"We have a three-day return policy, but few people ever use it," said Sharon. "Let me show you the dogs. Just beware. Some of them were mistreated and don't like anyone."

"Don't sound like they would be a good candidate for adoption," Roger said.

Sharon replied, "They're not. We normally have to put them down after the seven day waiting period. If no one wants them by then, they're history."

"It's a shame an animal has to suffer because someone was a jerk," Roger said.

"Yes, it is," Sharon said. "We see all kinds here, the vicious, the frightened, the lost. It can get you down if you let it, but I guess the county would be overrun if we weren't here."

They walked down a hallway with dogs in cages on both sides. One dog lunged as they walked. "Watch out for him. He's the last of a bunch of dogs a group used for fighting. Today's his last day."

They walked on past dogs of every description. Big, little, short legs, long legs, and every color of the dog rainbow it seemed. Sharon turned to Roger, "What exactly are you looking for?"

"I was thinking about a young German Shepherd or a good mix like that," Roger said.

Sharon put her fingers to her lips and patted them as she thought. "Hmmm," she said. "I think I have one you will like. We have a five-month-old female Shepherd mix that will get put down tomorrow if no one takes her. The bitch is really a nice dog, loving and attentive. Just waiting for the right person to come along to love and adopt her."

"Let me see her," Roger said. They walked around the corner and stopped in front of a cage with a young dog that looked like her breeding was German Shepherd and some other large breed of dog, maybe Chow. She got up from where she was lying, walked to the front of the cage, gave a little yelp/bark, and wagged her tail while looking at Roger. He put his fingers through the chain-link of the cage door. "Be careful," Sharon warned. "She could bite you."

Roger smiled and said, "I know what a dog that's gonna bite me looks like and this ain't one. Open the dog cage and let me get to know her better."

Sharon went into the cage, put a leash on the dog and led her out to Roger. He bent down on one knee and said, "Come here, girl. Come on over here."

She pulled at the leash and was soon giving Roger doggy kisses. He petted her entirely satisfied. "I'll take her," he said.

Sharon said, "Looks like you two were made for each other. She must have been someone's dog who got away and became lost. She was already spayed when she arrived, and with a few shots and twenty dollars to cover the shots, she's yours."

Roger said, "Sounds like a bargain to me. Let's go."

Bill Kenney had been watching all the goings-on without comment, until now. "Looks to me like you got yourself a fine animal there, Roger. I think you made a good choice."

"Yeah, I think I found me a winner. She's young, and I can teach her to be a guard dog, and she can keep the low life off my property," Roger said pointing at the officer when he said "low life." Bill smiled and said, "Yup, I think you found a keeper."

Roger Pyles paid the fee for the dog and signed some paperwork that Sharon gave him. She said, "It's been a long time since I seen a dog take to someone like she did to you. You saved her life. Tomorrow, we would have had to put her down."

"I think she will do just fine," Roger said. "Who knows? Maybe someday, she'll save mine."

"You never know, Mr. Pyles," Sharon said. "She may just do that; she may. You never know."

Roger looked at the dog accessories for sale. "How much is this dog bed? It looks well made."

Sharon said, "That will be twenty dollars, and it was made here in the county by the handicapped shelter. They take pride in their work."

"So I can see," Roger said. "Here's the twenty."

Sharon took the money and gave him a receipt. "Here you go and good luck with the dog. Got a name for her yet?"

Roger looked at her a little puzzled. "Why no, no I don't, but I'll think of something suitable." He began to walk away.

"And, Mr. Pyles?"

Roger turned to her. "What?"

"When you need another animal, we have lots of them and all kinds to adopt."

"Sure thing," Roger said to her. "I'll remember you guys here."

The two men walked to the truck, opened the door, and the dog hopped in, and sat on the bench seat between the men. "Looks like you got a good one, Roger. Let's get going. Mr. Crane will think we got lost."

"Hey, stop at McDonald's. Me and the dog need some lunch while we are out there," Roger said.

"Sure thing."

It was a short drive to the restaurant. They got two Quarter Pounders with fries and drinks, water for the dog and a Coke for Roger and were soon off again. Roger gave the dog some fries as they drove. When they pulled into the parking lot of the sales building for the development, the dog threw up with a mighty heave. Chief Kenney looked at Roger Pyles and swore. "Look what your dog just done to my truck!"

"Sorry," Roger said. "Guess she gets car sick." And he added, "It was your idea to get a dog first."

Bill Kenney swore again. "Don't remind me. You're gonna clean it up. I can't drive around with this smell all day. It'll make me sick."

"Okay," replied Roger. "I'll clean up the mess. When you've smelled as many dead and bloated bodies as I have, this ain't nothing."

Fortunately, Janet, the secretary at the office, had rags and towels for the cleanup. She told them Speedy would be waiting for them at the site. Roger made quick work of the dog puke. Bill Kenney growled at Roger and the dog. "You two are riding in the back. It smelled bad enough in the cab, and I don't want to see a repeat of puke everywhere. Got it?"

"Okay, chief. Whatever you say," Roger replied.

He put the young dog in the bed of the pickup and sat next to her. The two men and dog rode to the investigation site in silence. After a short, but bumpy drive down the rutted road, they arrived. At that moment, the dog rose up and a green-brown diarrhea shot from the dog's rear end and went all over the side of the truck bed. Chief

Kenney heard something, looked in the rearview mirror, saw the mess, and began to curse again. "Sorry, guess she didn't like your driving at all," Roger said. Bill spewed some more choice words to which Roger replied, "Don't worry. She didn't get it on the supplies. We'll unload them and use the bucket to wash the crap off. Okay?" Chief Kenney shook his head and nodded. Roger and the dog got out of the back of the truck.

Speedy came up to the truck. "Everything okay here?" he asked.

Roger said, "Dog didn't like the ride."

At that time, the aroma of the dog's leavings found Speedy's nose. Speedy looked at the irritated officer and the situation before him. "I see," was all he said.

Roger tied the dog's leash to a small shrub and then quickly unloaded the supplies from the back of the truck. He grabbed a bucket and headed for the water-filled ditch nearby. As he scooped up about four gallons of the black water, the radio in Bill's pickup truck squawked sharply, "Attention, Titusville Police have a 10-78 at I 95 and SR 50. All units in the area, please respond."

Chief Kenney grabbed the radio and said, "Canaveral Flats Unit 1 responding. Will be there in three minutes. Over."

"Canaveral Flats Unit 1, your assistance is appreciated. 10-10."

Chief Bill Kenney looked at the other two men. "Got to go." He hopped in the truck, backed up to turn around and began to head down the rutted dirt road toward Titusville.

"Hey!" yelled Roger Pyles. "What about the cleanout?"

"Have to wait till later," Bill Kenney yelled back and off he flew on the muddy road.

The two men watched the truck as it became smaller and smaller, and disappeared around a bend.

"Well," Roger said. "Guess it will have to wait. Wonder what a 10-78 is?"

Speedy said, "A 10-78 is an officer requesting assistance and send an ambulance. Usually bad news."

"Oh," Roger replied. "How did you know that?"

"My old man was a cop back in Michigan, where I came from. Cop codes down here are similar."

Roger was surprised, "So your father was a cop? A lot of cops want their sons to follow in their footsteps."

"Yeah, my dad did too. I was a lot like him, a real rebel growing up, and I raised a lot of hell growing up just like he did."

"I know," Roger said. "Seems to me some of the best cops were like that. They needed to get that out of their systems before they became the boys in blue."

Speedy said, "My dad and me never got along. We were too much alike. It was my granddad who raised me from my teens. I think he understood. If it wasn't for him, I wouldn't be here today."

Speedy had aroused Roger's curiosity. "Would you tell me more if it's not too personal?" Roger asked.

Speedy said, "It's personal, but I don't mind. My old man took the frustrations of his job out on Mom and me. He was one of those who couldn't separate his work from his home life. His drinking drove Mom away, and then he took it all out on me. Granddad got wind of what was going on, and he came and got me one day. I'd been getting into Dad's booze when he was at work and was a mess, too. Granddad got me interested in mechanics and heavy machinery and into the Operating Engineers Union when I became eighteen. It was a hellish time in my life. I wrecked two cars while drunk. Dad finally tired of his life and ended it with a bullet to the head from his service gun. After that, I was so low I could have crawled under a closed door. At the age of twenty, I found myself sitting on a hay bale in Granddad's barn with a gun in my hand and planned on ending the pain. It was like I heard a voice in my head saying, 'Like father, like son.' Granddad found me there and talked me out of it. He told me how he'd felt as low as one time in his life, but couldn't go through with killing himself. The twelve-step program, meeting my grandma, and getting a job gave him meaning and the will to continue."

Speedy was quiet for a moment and began again, "I sat there with that gun in my hand and thought about what he said. He did not know if I would do it or maybe even shoot the two of us."

"I handed him the gun. He embraced me, and I cried like a baby, a hurting baby at that. I owe my life to that man."

Roger whistled through his teeth. "That's a heavy-duty story. One I hadn't expected."

Speedy said, "Yeah, walk a mile in my shoes before you think you know and judge me."

Roger nodded, and Speedy spoke again, "Shortly afterward, I met my wife at a Harley rally, and the rest is history. With my troubles with the law, I could never have become a cop, but the operators and construction companies didn't care as long as I did good work on the job. Granddad said my old man had been just as bad, but in the old days, things could get covered up if you knew the right people. Glad I did become an operator. Like Granddad said, I was too much like my dad, and I think I would have ended up the same way if I had followed in his footsteps. It takes a special kind of person to deal with the world at its worst and not let it get to you. I salute those that can. Well, enough about me. I probably bored you to tears with my story."

Roger replied, "No, not at all. It's good when a man finally faces his biggest enemy, usually himself, and conquers him." Roger thought of himself as he said that.

Speedy said, "Let me show you some things that will help you here. I'm gonna need to get back to work." He walked over to the large pump that had the big pipe, which led to the dewatering well points. "If it starts getting soupy or you see water rising in the drained area, flip the red switch up, and the pump motor will fire up. Flip it down when it starts sucking air to turn it off, okay? The automatic sensor for this isn't working, so it's manual or nothing till we get it fixed."

"Got it. Seems simple enough. What else?" asked Roger.

"Be careful where you walk. The muck has been known to suck off a boot or worse," Speedy said. He looked at him and continued, "Over where that highest black point is, is where I started my last scoop with the big backhoe. I think if there's more than a hand in there, you'll find remains somewhere under and below that. I think the skulls came from a little lower down in the swamp, but I could be wrong on that. Not exactly sure which of the last scoops they were in, but if I was a betting man, I would say everything came up in the last big scoop of muck. That's the best I can do. Do you have any questions?"

Roger asked, "Do you have a two-way radio? If I find something more, I'll need to call the coroner for a pickup. Human remains won't last long in this heat. We have to work fast."

Speedy spoke, "I don't have an extra to spare, but Mr. Crane said to give you mine so you can call his office if need be. The office will relay any messages to whoever we need."

Roger nodded approval. "One last question, why do they call you Speedy? That's not your real name is it?"

"No, my given name is Stefan, but I much prefer Speedy," he said. "I like to race cars over at Orlando Speed World in the beautiful town of Bithlo, also known as Junkyardville. Someone, who I can't remember, gave me the nickname when I was winning numerous races and the name stuck."

"Well, Speedy, thanks for your help," Roger said. "Looks like I need to get to work." Roger walked closer to the site before him. The hunt for answers would begin, and like so many times, he would soon be amazed at where it would take him.

Chapter 7

Roger Pyles watched as Speedy's truck got smaller and smaller as it bumped down the muddy road. It disappeared around a bend. He looked at his canine companion who had also been watching the truck, and said, "Little dog with no name, looks like it's just you and me, the skeeters, and whatever is in that muck."

Roger smiled and laughed to himself as a song came into his head. Where and why it had come, he didn't know, but the rock band America and "Horse with No Name" was playing in his head. He began to sing to the dog, "Oh, I'm out in the swampland with a dog with no name." He looked at the sky. "I sure hope it doesn't rain. If it does, I'll have water on the brain, and I won't be able to remember my own name, let alone, the name of a dog with no name. La la, la la la la, la la la la."

Roger stopped singing and said, "Dog with no name, we have got to get you a name, or it with drive me insane. It's a thang I won't have to explain here in the swampland, not the desert in the rain." Roger shook his head, "What do you know? I'm a poet who doesn't know it."

The dog with no name gave a happy bark. Roger smiled, went, and petted the dog. He said, "Even my horrible singing must be better than being locked in a cage with a death sentence waiting for you, dog. Guess I could be locked up too at the drunk tank. Maybe we're both lucky on that and lucky to have each other's company."

The dog gave another happy bark, and Roger patted her head some more. "I better get to work. If I find something, and I think I will, it could be a long day."

He got the camera, took some pictures of the area he would search, and made some notes he'd need later. Speedy was right about the muck. It would suck your boots off. Carefully, he walked around the site and tested the peaty muck for resistance. Some spots were soft, while others were rather tough. A shovel would work at the rough cutting through the fibrous material, and a smaller garden spade, a kitchen dish brush, and the sprayer should work on the more delicate tasks ahead.

Roger looked over the site. He was able to visualize what Speedy had told him about his last use of the big machine's bucket. The peaty muck, scarred from the teeth of the backhoe, and a thin film of black debris from the swamp covered everything. With the sprayer, he washed this away best he could. A plan was coming together. He made his way to the top and noted the difference in the textured composition of peat he had stepped on. It was firm, but a place the size of a small grave seemed a little less firm and the place to begin his search.

He pulled out the camera and took some more pictures. He would do this throughout his work here. The old adage about a picture being worth a thousand words was very accurate, especially in court cases.

Speedy's backhoe had cut a bank with about a thirty-degree angle on it, and Roger began to dig with the shovel. The peat was tough and heavy, but he noted the shovel cut into it with less resistance than an undisturbed area a few feet away. He had used that area for a test spot to know what to expect from the sinewy material.

Clearly, this grave-shaped area had been dug up and then refilled with the same matter. It no longer had a homogeneous texture, but one that appeared mixed. It did not require nearly as much effort to dig into the disturbed black humus. As carefully as he could, he worked his way down through the coal-colored earth and piled it nearby to look at later for any evidence it may contain. About three feet down, his shovel hit something different. It was softer than the coarse humus, and Roger felt he had found the body to which the arm and hand belonged.

He removed as much earth as practical with the shovel and looked in the hole he had dug. There was definitely something there, and it appeared human, a naked back specifically. Roger grabbed the sprayer and squirted water on the body to clean it off. To his surprise, it did not seem to have decomposed at all, if any. He'd read of how a body buried quickly after death, where oxygen was not present remained relatively intact, but this was the first time he had seen it firsthand. While in Europe some years ago, he had seen the thousand-year-old remains of people buried in bogs. This body had been stained brown, he believed, from the tannins in the soils.

As he uncovered more of the body, he found a rope around the neck, and he was now sure the body was female and entirely naked except for a necklace with a distinct charm which hung to the cleavage of her ample breasts. At the top was a menorah with a Star of David attached below, followed by something that resembled a fish hanging down. He'd seen something like this before, but he could not remember where. She appeared young and probably had blond hair, but it was hard to tell because of the tannins' coloration. Her eyes bulged somewhat. He suspected strangulation with the rope.

One arm was behind her back and remains of duct tape were visible on the remaining hand's wrist. He could see where the teeth on the backhoe bucket had severed the other arm. If Speedy's machine had cut the earth any deeper, it would have torn the body to pieces. Roger cleared more dirt away and made another discovery; her pubic hair was missing, shaved clean. The body appeared to have been positioned in the hole. In his mind, Roger could imagine a man controlling her from behind with the rope and raping her doggy style. The coroner could check her neck to see if his idea was correct or not. The rope would make a distinct pattern he should find on a close examination of her neck, and perhaps the hyoid bone would show signs of trauma also.

Roger had seen gruesome death before, yet the cold-blooded actions mankind was capable of, never ceased to disgust him. And this woman looked to be about the same age and build as his late wife. "Poor lady," he said. "I'll do whatever I can to find out who the bastard was that did this to you."

He stopped for a moment and reached for the radio Speedy had given him. Roger pressed on the button and said, "Hello, this is Roger Pyles over at the dig site. Is anybody there?"

"Roger, this is Janet over at the office. What do you need?"

"Janet, I need you to get in touch the county coroner pronto. I found the body that went with the hand. It's a young woman who I think was strangled." He left out the part about suspecting rape. The coroner should be able to determine that in his examining room far better than Roger could in the mucky swamp. "She's not in bad shape considering, but this heat will kick decomposition into overdrive rapidly, so he needs to get out here ASAP. And tell him he needs something with four-wheel-drive to get back here."

"I'll do that," she said. "How are you holding out?"

Roger understood the double meaning. "I've got water and some munchies out here for me and the dog, and if you're wondering, in the police work I've done back up north in the past, I've seen a lot of dead bodies." He left out the part about feeling revolted by the similarities to his dead wife. "Tell him to get out here now before the evidence goes south."

"Understood," she said. "I'll call him, explain the urgency of the matter and get back with you as soon as I have something."

"Okay, Janet. Let me know whatever he says."

"Will do. Out."

"And out here, too," Roger said to himself out loud.

Roger looked at the partially uncovered body in front of him. "Well, young lady, if there's anything you can do to help me find out who did this to you, please help me."

He did not expect an answer from her, but he knew that often the answer was there right in front of him. All he had to do was put the pieces of the puzzle together. Roger continued to separate the body from the earth and spray it down to clean it off.

"Roger?" rattled the radio. "Roger? Are you there?"

Roger grabbed the radio. "Yeah, I'm here. What did you find out?"

"Coroner says he's on the way from Melbourne in the county four-wheel-drive GMC Safari. His ETA should be within the hour."

"Thanks, Janet. That's better than I expected. I've got the body almost completely uncovered and should be ready to turn her over to him when he arrives."

"Okay, if there are any more developments, I'll pass them on to you as soon as I get them."

"Thanks again, Janet. Mr. Crane needs to give you a raise."

"I know he does, but jobs are scarce now with this recession. That idiot Carter did this, and I was dumb enough to fall for his malarkey, only once, though."

"Whatever you say, Janet." Roger didn't think there was usually a dime's difference between politicians of any of the parties, but he kept this to himself. "Call me if you have anything new."

"Roger that, Roger, and out," she said.

"Roger out here too."

Roger laid the radio down and went back to work. He uncovered more of the body and looked at it in the awkward doggy sex position. "Wish you could tell me more who done this to you." He gently sprayed more water on the hand. Roger thought there may still be evidence under her fingernails. Perhaps she had scratched her killer. As he uncovered more of her fingers, something dropped from her hand. It was covered in mud, and Roger picked it up in his glove covered hands. He rolled it in his palm and poured some water on it. It appeared to be a piece of jewelry or something like it. He picked it up in his fingers and scrutinized it. It seemed to have two stylized letters on it. *Could it be SS? Yes*, he thought, *it did say SS. Someone's initials or something else?* He'd have to find out. Perhaps the dead woman had heard him and given him the clue or at least a clue he needed. Maybe. It would be up to him and others to find out.

He placed the item in a small plastic bag and put this in his shirt pocket. Roger had found nothing else to collect, but he still wanted to sieve the muck and peat mixture he had dug from around the body for additional clues. At that time he heard the dog with no name give out a short growl and then a short guttural bark. She was looking off into the vast swamp.

Roger looked off in the direction the dog observed but could see nothing. He had an eerie feeling he was being watched, but by whom or what, he could not tell. Roger saw only the densely vegetated swampland that moved with the wind. "Easy girl," he said. "Do you see something?"

The dog barked louder this time and turned her attention to Roger, who carefully walked to where the dog was tied. "What did you see, dog with no name? I couldn't see anything, but I think there was something there. What was it? A man? Coyote? Maybe the

Swamp Ape?" Roger had heard stories of hermits living in the St. John River marshes which this most assuredly connected. Some of the tales were of escaped criminals on the lamb while others were of Seminole Indians gone native. Still, others were of war veterans, usually from the Vietnam War, who could not adjust to life back in the "civilized" world and had left it for this wild area of gators, wild pigs, and snakes of all sorts, though the aggressive cottonmouth was most feared. The small dog just looked at him, and Roger noted her tongue was hanging out.

"Don't know what it was, but you keep a lookout, okay?"

The dog gave a little yelp when he said that. "Bet you're thirsty. I know I am." He grabbed a bottle of water from the nearby supplies and took a big swig. "My, that's good. Warm, but good and I bet you want some."

The dog barked in agreement and Roger found a suitable container for a doggy bowl for her water which she lapped up greedily. "Maybe that was the problem or at least part of it."

He looked over at the naked body nearly freed from the muck. "Sure hope that coroner gets here on time. Now that I've got her almost out, she won't last long in the Florida heat." He stopped and then said, "You know, dog with no name, I think I've been away from people too long because here I'm talking to you like you were another human and expecting you to answer." He shook his head. "Guess I better get back to work and see what else I can find that'll help us solve this mystery. Young women don't end up like this without someone's help and I, for one, want to see justice done."

The dog gave out a yelp as if she understood. "No wonder you're known as man's best friend. I need to get back to work." He walked gingerly back through the muck to where the body was. The camera was in the bucket where he left it, and he took some more pictures that could be used for evidence later. With the shovel, he removed the rest of the humus material near the lower part of the victim's body and piled it on the growing heap. So far, nothing in it had caught his eye, but something could be hidden that a proper screening would find. He knew the importance of not missing evidence from past cases he had worked for the police while up north. One little discovery could make or break a case, a fact he remembered well.

After that, he brushed away the black material from the body and used the sprayer to clean her. At that time, he noticed a small rose tattoo on her now exposed ankle. He got the camera and took several shots of it. Perhaps this was the clue that could confirm her identity. Roger doubted if there were too many missing young women with tattoos of any kind on their ankles from this area.

Roger looked back at his new dog, the dog with no name as of yet, and found she was lying down, her eyes closed, and she appeared to be sleeping. *Guess all the excitement done tuckered her out. That and she may not be feeling too well after the purge from both ends.*

Roger continued digging around the body and spraying her clean with the sprayer, but he found nothing new. He heard the dog bark and looked to see an official-looking van coming down the pothole-filled road. As the white GMC Safari van got closer, Roger could read Brevard County Coroner painted on it along with a picture of the Space Shuttle. Brevard County was the home to Kennedy Space Center from where America's race into space had begun. The county had seen its ups and downs depending on the support the program had from the President and Congress. Things were on the upswing now with President Reagan and Congress firmly behind the new Shuttle program.

The driver stopped the van and got out. He was a portly man with thick lenses in the black plastic glasses. His head was bald on top, but the hair on the sides was long and scraggly, and he had a scruffy ponytail which went halfway down his back.

The dog with no name barked as he called out, "Guess you must be that new Canaveral Flats officer, Roger Pyles, they told me to look for. I'm Will Corbett, coroner of this fine county and it looks like you have a body for me."

"You hit the nail on the head there, partner," Roger said. "You got the name right, and this is our victim. Come on over here, but be careful where you step. Some places don't seem to have a bottom."

"Thanks for the warning. It's not my first adventure in Florida swamps, but it always pays to know where to step. Learned that in Vietnam. Saw one idiot blown sky-high when he refused to stay in the lead soldier's footsteps near Pleiku. That landmine did a number on him and injured several others in the vicinity. Some people have to learn the hard way, and because they're so hard-headed, others get hurt too."

"Watch that area over there," Roger said, and he pointed to a spot ten feet away. "Liked to sucked off a boot before I could retreat."

"Will do," the coroner said as he advanced toward Roger. "Let's see what we have here. Hmm. What appears to be a probably white, but maybe not, definitely female and naked, missing a hand and part of her arm, buried in a hole, with a rope around her neck. Hmm. I think we can rule out suicide and natural causes. People don't normally kill themselves naked. I'd say we have a murder on our hands and recent. Minimal decomposition. We'll know more when I get her back to the lab and do a complete examination."

"Where did you learn your coroner skills?" Roger asked.

"Why, back in Vietnam. Shortly after that fool like to got me killed with the landmine, I heard they were looking for men to help in the mortuary on base, so I jumped on it. I figured I was a whole lot safer working with the dead than in the infantry in the jungle with an enemy in it wanting to kill me and halfwits on our side trying to do the same. It really toughened me up, so this is nothing today. Usually, the bodies stink to high heavens and the ants, maggots, and heat have done a number on the bodies."

Roger said, "I got drafted into this job." He didn't go into details. "I helped solve some cases up north in the area where Maryland, West Virginia, Pennsylvania, and Virginia all come together. I was a professor up there at Western Maryland University, but that's another story, too. And I agree. This is nothin'. Worst case I ever saw was a girl's body that had turned to 'soup.' It was sloshing around in the body bag, and we had to try to find the cause of death. I don't think anyone, including me, kept his lunch down that day, except the senior coroner. It didn't seem to faze him."

Coroner Will nodded. "Seen some like that. Blew my lunch too on the first one, but now not much affects me. This one is a beauty. Looks like you done a good job uncovering her. What happened to the missing hand?"

"Backhoe took it off. That's how they found her," Roger said.

"Oh, yeah. Brought that in along with two discolored skulls. The skulls looked ancient to me, so I sent them up to the guys at Florida State in Tallahassee to examine. It looks like I'll be able to reunite the hand with its owner back at the lab. How stiff and squishy is she?"

Roger replied, "Not stiff at all, but very flexible, and she should hold together when we move her."

"Excellent," the coroner said. "I had one, an asphyxiation suicide in a car in a garage over in Satellite Beach last week that had been in the heat for three days before someone discovered her. You can smell them before you get there. When I pulled on her fat arm to get her out of the car, it came off. What a mess that was."

Roger nodded, "Yeah, death is not pretty whether it's an animal or a human."

"Agreed. If you're interested in that kind of stuff, I can arrange for you to visit the Body Farm they have over near Tampa. There are several across the country, but conditions with the extreme heat and rain in this state make for some unique body decomposition patterns not seen in other places."

"Yeah, I understand what you are saying," Roger replied. "I've been to the Body Farm near Knoxville, Tennessee, but I think I'll pass on it for now. A rain check for later will work fine."

"Okay, we need to quit jawin' and get this woman to a cool place like my morgue in Melbourne. I'll get us some Tyvek lab coats to protect our clothes when we carry her down to the sheet we will cover her with."

"Sounds like a plan," Roger said.

Coroner Will warily made his way back to his van, got out a flat gurney board, placed it on the ground as close to the swampy area as he could. There he laid a large, open white sheet on it. He went back to the van, found two Tyvek lab suits, and walked over to Roger and the body. "Put this on. I think we need to stretch her out. If you get her under the arms, I'll take the legs, and we will slowly proceed to the gurney and place her there."

"Sounds like you've done this often," Roger said.

Will rolled his eyes. "All too often. I wish Death would take a day off."

"My wife used to tell me she longed for the day when Death would die," Roger said.

Will lamented, "We can only hope for that day, but then I would have to find another job." He looked at Roger and said, "I think I'd like the change."

"How right you are."

The two men put on the protective coats and gloves. The little dog barked as she watched the two men.

"Roger said, "How do you like my new dog? She has a weak stomach, but I think she will work out fine."

"Weak stomach? How so?"

"We came over with Chief Kenney of the Canaveral Flats Police Department. She threw up all over the truck cab, so he demanded we ride in the back bed. We did and then she crapped all over it. I got the puke cleaned up, but he got a call before I could clean up the back and took off on a call."

"Now that's funny. I would love to have seen that. What's her name?"

Roger replied, "I haven't given her a name yet. I want one that suits her, so for now, she's the dog with no name."

"Like that song by the band, America – "The Horse with No Name"?"

"That's the one."

Will looked at Roger and asked, "So are you the doctor they've been talking about?"

"Who?"

"The one from up north who moved down here after some real hard luck."

Roger sighed, "That's probably me. I fit that description big time."

"Well, Doctor Who, why don't you name her K9 like in the British TV show?"

The dog barked at that. "See," said Will. "She likes it."

"I believe you're right. Well, dog with no name, looks like you're now officially K9."

The dog, formerly known as the dog with no name, barked and seemed to give a doggy smile.

Will said, "Looks like it's K9," and he paused, "Doctor."

"Okay, okay, thought you were eager to get the body to the cool morgue."

"Right, let's do it. You grab her around the armpits, and I'll take the legs. We'll go real slow. It's slippery and sloping down to the gurney. Let's do this right the first time."

"Agreed," Roger said.

The two men worked the body from its crouching, leapfrog-like position, onto its back. They carried her as they had planned through the slick area to the gurney on the ground while the dog, now known as K9, attentively watched. As carefully as they could, they laid the woman's body down face up on the wooden, sheet-covered gurney.

"That went easier than I expected," the coroner said Will. "She ain't in too bad a shape compared to most I have seen like this. Looks like she was a pretty thing about mid-20, I'd say. Well-built with a small rose tattoo on the ankle, and she liked to shave down there. Never could figure out why women did that."

"Me neither. My late wife did too. I told her it made her look like a little girl."

Will laughed and asked, "What did she say to that?"

"She wiggled her cute little nose a little annoyed and said she was already shaving her legs and armpits, so why not there?"

Will chuckled, "Yeah, why not? It's hard to argue with that female logic."

"Agreed," Roger said. "She could turn into a real animal in the bedroom shaved or not."

"Can't they all? What happened to her?" asked Will.

Roger was silent for a moment. He sighed and said, "She died in an auto accident along with our young son. I really miss them. I wanted to die when they did. It crushed the life out of me, and I've been here ever since. Jim Beam, Jack Daniels or Wild Turkey or whatever, have been my constant companions. I could use a drink right now." He pulled a small flask from his pocket and took a swig. "Ah, alcohol. It does a body good. Care for a swig?"

The coroner looked like he wished he had never asked the question. "No," he responded. "I'm on duty. Don't want to lose my job. I know others do it, but I only drink what little I do, after work. Thanks anyway."

46

The coroner covered up the body tucked the sheets firmly around it and tied it in place with straps. He got a cart from the van and set it up just outside. He looked at Roger. "How about giving me a hand? We'll set the wooden gurney on the cart, and I'll slide it in the van. It's designed for that and will make it easier for me down at the morgue."

"Sure," Roger said.

The process went like clockwork, and the two men walked to the front of the van.

Coroner Will said, "Thanks for your help. I'll get back with you ASAP with the results of my investigation. Let's see if we can't find the killer." Roger nodded. "And sorry if I asked too many questions about your wife. One of the bad habits you develop in this business. You're always looking for answers."

"No harm done," said Roger. "I've been holding this in too long, and it just came out like a tidal wave. It should be me apologizing for putting you on the spot."

"No problem," Will said. "I best be goin' before my cargo starts to spoil. Again, I'll call you when I have some results from her autopsy. Got to go. Bye."

Roger stopped him and said, "Now you have her in your care, I can ask this. The county sheriff's department wouldn't help me with the investigation, told my chief we were on our own, and here you are helping. What's up?"

Will smiled, "First off, I heard about the spat you all were having, but fact is, I work for the County Commission like the sheriff does, and if they decided that I should not help, I haven't got the memo, but then I'm always dead last, pun intended, when it comes to getting information from them."

Roger laughed at the pun. "Gotcha. You heard nothing just like Sergeant Schultz on Hogan's Heroes."

"Yup, a little gallows humor too, to keep me from going crazy. Hey, got to go. See you. Bye."

Roger said, "Bye," and waved. Will got into the van, turned around, and then disappeared down the mucky road. Roger turned to his furry companion and said, "Well, dog with no name," he stopped, "I mean, K9, looks like I need to get back to work and see what else I can find of interest here about the body or the old bones

Speedy found. Just wondering where this puzzle will lead us." He looked at the dewatered search area. "Somehow, I don't think all the pieces are visible yet, and they may never be. Let's see if we can figure out what it is with what we got, right, K9?"

There was no response. Roger's eyes turned to the dog, and he saw she was lying down with her eyes closed. "Too much excitement for one day and with that purge, guess you don't feel well, K9. You get some rest and, no, if I find any more bones, you don't get one to chew on."

K9 sighed once, and her eyes went closed like shutters before a storm.

Roger spoke to the dog, but more to himself. "Looks like the Do Not Disturb sign is up. I get the hint." He walked over to the search area and spoke to no one in particular. "Let's see what there is to find. I think I'm going to be surprised."

Chapter 8

Roger Pyles looked around the swamp and then at the sky. There were very few clouds even though this was usually the rainy season, but it was scorching. Some clouds and some rain would cool the heat down, but there was little chance of that today. Roger was glad for this as he had no shelter if it did storm and he did not know when his friend, Chief of Police Bill Kenney, was coming back. For all he knew, Chief Kenney would wait till after the storm was over to come to pick him up and the dog now known as K9. The Canaveral Flats cop was probably still steamed about the dog's accidents in his truck.

Roger thought for a moment. *When had the crime occurred?* Speedy had mentioned earlier that the access road to the spot where he was, had only existed for about a month and a half. Roger knew it had rained heavily about a month ago and the new gumbo road would not have been passable by anything but a tracked vehicle after that. Since then, only a few drops had fallen, and Roger wondered why this particular area was as wet as it was. *A spring, perhaps*? He would have to look into that further. *Was there something different about this place?*

The killer, if it was a murder, could have driven here and done his dirty deed before the rain made this road impossible to drive on. He would try to keep an open mind on this even when the evidence all pointed to murder. Roger had seen how easily cops and the feds developed tunnel vision when they were on the trail. His finding and evidence had blown at least one open-and-shut case out of the water when he lived up north. Several of the cops had not forgiven him, even though as he had pointed out, he was only doing his job to the best of his abilities just as they were. The ideal time for this event would be a month ago. He knew a body completely buried in a peat bog would decompose very differently from one dumped in a watery swamp in this state. He'd seen what bodies buried in peat for thousands of years looked like while in Europe years ago. Still, if it was a month ago, he had expected more decay. Something was not right, and he knew he needed to understand why. You could possibly get here on horseback in a severe drought year, but horses were not exactly the vehicle of choice now. A truck would be more likely.

He looked around again. The feeling of being watched was back, but he could see nothing. The little dog continued to sleep. "Fine watchdog you are," he said. At that, K9 opened her eyes slightly, gave out a short sigh, and went back to sleep. Roger shook his head. *Maybe he only imagined it,* but he couldn't shake the feeling. Feeling or no feeling, he had work to do. He would exercise caution himself and watch the dog closely. She should hear or smell anything long before he would.

Roger was interested in looking where Speedy had told him to check for the old bones, but the young woman's case must take priority. He would look for additional evidence left behind and sift through the muck he'd removed from around the body. The task occupied him for nearly two hours, but to his disappointment, he found nothing new. Edmond Locard, the French man who was the father of forensic crime scene investigation, was the first to point out that something was always left behind by the doer or doers of crimes. No matter how wiped clean the scene was, something was still left. All they had to do was find it, figure out what they had, and then pursue it wherever the evidence led them. It sounded simple and was, but many things could and probably would go wrong in the investigation. The point was never to quit, and like Sherlock Holmes, one of his favorite characters in books had said, "When you eliminate the impossible, whatever remains, no matter how improbable, must be the truth."

This young woman, nude and buried with a rope around her neck, had not got there without help and he intended to find out who had helped her get where she was. Roger knew why he was taking this personal. The dead woman resembled his late wife. And this young woman with the rose tattoo on her ankle deserved justice.

The whole time Roger worked, the little dog had slept. Roger still felt he was being watched. The only evidence he had found was the body that appeared to be placed in the grave with the rope around the neck and the little pin. Some murderers were convicted with less evidence, but all he had was what he had, and he would have to work with this. Roger hoped it was enough.

The sleeping dog awoke and rose. She gave a little bark. Roger turned toward her, gasped and standing no more than six feet from him was a brown-skinned man wearing a native breechcloth and little more. He had a rope tied like a bandanna around his head that kept his long hair in place, and he carried a menacing-looking spear in his right hand. He spoke, "The Ancient Ones are angry at what has happened. You must make it right."

The startled Roger could not find words. The dark-skinned man looked at the dog, nodded and spoke again, "Canine say thank you for saving her life. Maybe someday, she can return the favor." He walked around Roger, looked at the hole, and shook his head. At this time the dog looked down the road, growled, and then barked. Roger turned and saw Chief Bill Kenney's truck's nose coming around a corner down the muddy lane. He turned to the dark-skinned man, but he was not there. He'd vanished. The truck and driver continued coming closer, came to a halt, and stopped near where the dog was tied. Chief of Police Bill Kenney got out and walked toward Roger Pyles. The dog barked again at the cop.

The Chief of Police asked Roger, "Well, how are you doin', ole buddy. You look a little shell-shocked."

Roger nodded, "A native-looking man just appeared behind me, left a cryptic message, and then as quickly as he came, vanished when we heard the sound of your truck."

"The Shaman," Bill Kenney said. "You met the Shaman. That's what they call him. I don't know his real name."

"Who's the Shaman?" Roger asked.

"I've never met him myself," Bill Kenney replied, "but I know of him. Lots of stories about him floating around. Some true. Some wild exaggerations. Best I can figure, he's a Seminole Indian from their big reservation down south gone native. Some say he's a medicine man who lives by the old ways. Others say he's some kind of a spirit who moves like the wind and watches like a phantom over all the area of the St. Johns River drainage. I've never seen him, but those that have, never forget the experience."

"You can say that again. He sure got my attention," Roger said. "Is he crazy or threatening?"

"From the stories I've heard, he talks to the animals, the sky and the wind. I think that's a little strange. Did he do something like that while here or threaten you?"

Roger let out a little whistle. "He frightened me, but he wasn't threatening. He made no moves toward harming me, but he did do some weird things."

"Like what?"

"He said, 'The Ancient Ones are angry at what has happened. You must make it right.'"

Bill Kenney raised his eyebrows. "That is weird. Wonder if he meant the murder or the bones being disturbed or both?"

Roger shrugged his shoulders. "I don't know, but we need to find out who killed the girl," and he added, "and I think we need to treat any more bones we find with respect."

"Agreed," Bill Kenney said. "Did he say anything more?"

"Yeah, he called my dog K9, that's the name I gave her. Don't know how he knew that, but he said she thanked me for saving her life and she would try to do the same for me."

"Like I told you about this Shaman fellow, Roger, he dances to a different drummer and flute and seems to see things. I'll say this, you've saved her twice. I wanted to brain her when she soiled my truck. I think she owes you big time."

"Okay, I think I heard enough about this Shaman character, boss man. Did you take care of the emergency? What was the problem?"

The chief's continence changed, and he growled, "It was a cluster from the start. Rookie Titusville cop gave out the wrong code. He was looking for a simple backup, and half of north Brevard County cops descended on the spot when they thought he was in trouble. Then, some idiot drove up and ran into one of the cars. The driver was so drunk or drugged up, he could barely walk, and then he got into a fight with us. Took four men to get him down on the ground and cuff him. And then another car ignored an officer's direction, and T-boned yet another car that spun and took out a fire hydrant."

"Gee," Roger said. "That sounds pretty bad. Don't think it could get any worse."

"It did, and it's your fault."

"But I wasn't there. I didn't do nothin'."

"Oh, yes you did. The guys started complaining about how bad it smelled, and one of them followed the stench to the back of my truck," the chief growled. "They made all kinds of crude remarks, and the worst of it was, they started calling me Stinky. Don't know if I will live this down, but it's your fault and cops have long memories. Hope it doesn't stick. Thanks, old buddy."

"Sorry," Roger said. "I did get the dog puke cleaned up in the cab and would have gotten to the crap in the truck bed if you hadn't left here like a bat outta hell."

Bill grunted, and they both stood in silence after venting their built-up tensions.

"Don't smell bad now," Roger said.

Bill responded, "Yeah, after the razzing and we got traffic and things back to normal, I stopped at a car wash and used the wand to wash everything off."

"Bet the attendant at the car wash was not happy with you."

"He hardly even noticed I was there. Some joker had been there before the attendant showed up in the morning and had hosed down a 4x4 swamp buggy. There was stuff everywhere."

"Stuff? You said stuff," questioned Roger. "You usually use a more colorful word than stuff. What gives? You tryin' to turn over a new leaf?"

Bill shrugged his shoulders. "Something like that. The new kinder gentler me. Besides, it was stuff as in plural. There were mud and muck all over the place, and he'd had dogs with him too, so it was more than just sh…"

Roger cut him off. "Yeah, you were right on the word. The plural is stuff. I think I remember going over that in seventh grade English class at our old school."

"Yeah," Bill said. "Those were some good days. That was right before the sh…; I mean stuff hit the fan in my young life."

"Yes," Roger replied. "I remember your mother's death. Sad and so young."

"I remember it like it was yesterday. I walked into the house and found her lying on the floor. Just a spot of blood the size of a quarter on the floor. Doctors said her heart just stopped, and it was all over for Mom."

"And that's when you moved down here with your dad for good."

Bill said, "Yup. That about sums it up. You know how he left after the divorce. He took the job of Chief of Police in Canaveral Flats, and I took his place when his sickness started to get the worst of him. Black lung from the mines and years of smoking finally caught up with him. Sad how I lost both parents before they were 45."

Roger said nothing. He turned his head away as Bill appeared to wipe a tear from his eye. After a moment, Bill spoke. "So, what have you and this dog with no name, I mean K9, with nothing in her gut found out? I see you have been doing some serious diggin'."

"Yeah, while you were out by Interstate 95 saving the world, me and K9, but mainly me, have been busy. There was a young woman's body buried in that hole you see, and she was missing part of her arm."

"What else?" Bill Kenney asked now sounding official.

"She was naked, appeared to be posed in the grave like in kind of a leapfrog position, but with her butt in the air so to speak, had a rope around her neck, and I found duct tape on her wrist, the only one she had still connected."

The chief whistled through his teeth. "Sounds to me like a murder. You don't have to be a rocket scientist to figure that out, even though we have a bunch available nearby."

"I concur," Roger said.

"Yes, I think she was killed about a month ago just before the one big rain we had. Speedy gave me information on the road construction in the area that makes me think it had to be then. I was expecting more decomposition of the body, but the flesh decays differently in peat bogs like this. And there's still something going on here I can't put my finger on."

"How so?"

"Like I said, think there should have been more decay of the body, and one more thing."

"What's that?"

"I had this feeling of being watched the whole time."

Bill replied, "Yeah, the Shaman. I know that feeling. Seems like it's quite common with people who do law enforcement. Trust your feelings on this and stay alert while you are here," and as an afterthought, he added, "be careful. You never know where an investigation like this will take you or what danger it can put you in. It can spring out of nowhere and get you, so beware."

Roger nodded. "I sieved through the earth that was around the body and found nada, but oh, I did find this item." Roger pulled the small plastic bag with the pin in it from his shirt pocket and handed it to his boss. The chief took it and looked closely at it. "Ever see anything like that before?"

The chief said, "Yeah, I think I have, but I can't remember where right now. It looks familiar, but I'm gonna have to think about it. Why don't you take it over to the library and ask? Those people are a wealth of information most in our community overlook."

Roger said, "I'll do that and hope you remember too."

The chief held the plastic bag in his fingers before Roger. "Tell me where you found this."

"As I was digging the body out of the peat, it fell out of her hand."

The chief whistled. "That's important. It may be the clue we need to crack this."

"I hope so," Roger said. "I sure hope so."

"Give me your summary of what happened here, Mr. Expert."

Roger winced at that. "I wish you would not call me that even if it is true." He paused, "My best theory at this time is it happened a month ago. This woman was stripped, raped, and strangled with a rope around her neck. The man had sex with her from behind as he was controlling her and slowly strangling her to death. Her wrists were duct-taped behind her, and somehow she managed to grab that pin in her hand as he was doing his sick act on her."

"You got all that from this?" Bill Kenney gestured to the crime scene.

"Yes," he said, "as you so rightfully pointed out, I am an expert on this sort of thing."

"And worth every penny I'm paying you," the chief said.

"Speaking of pay, I could use some, Mr. El Cheapo."

The chief looked at him sternly and said, "If this can help get you sober and out of that drunken funk you've been in for the last year you've been here, you should be paying me for giving you purpose and helping put your life back together. That's worth more than money."

Roger lowered his eyes and nodded. The chief was right, he knew, but Roger grumbled under his breath that a little money would be good too. Roger knew the chief had heard, but his boss said nothing more.

Finally, the chief broke the silence, "I got some ideas on how to get some money, but I'd rather not talk about it now. So you named her Canine?"

"Yup," he said, "she's K9."

"I know she's a canine. What's her name?"

"K9," Roger said. "Her name is K9."

"What?"

"Did you ever watch the Doctor show on TV?"

"Who?"

"Yup, that's the one."

"Who?" asked the chief.

"Yes, you know, 'Doctor Who.'"

"What?"

"Not what, Who, 'Doctor Who,' that science fiction show on British TV.

"I think I am beginning to understand," said the chief. "Doctor Who, the TV character and he had a dog named Canine. Is that correct?"

"What?"

"Okay, I surrender. This is beginning to sound like an Abbott and Costello routine?"

"What?"

Officer Kenney replied, "He's on second. Who's on first."

"Who's on first?" Roger asked.

"Right, Who's on first, What's on second."

"I don't give a darn," Roger answered.

"He's the shortstop."

"Who?"

"Who's on first."

"Okay, I give up. I know when I've been outclassed in the joker department. I was trying to tell you, **Chief of Police Kenney**, that the dog's name is K9 as in the letter K and the number nine. The coroner said the dog with no name needed a name and it was his idea of K9. He pointed out I was a doctor and the Doctor on TV, Doctor Who, had a dog named K9."

"Who?" asked the officer.

"That's right. Now you're getting with the program, Doctor Who, not Doctor What, or I Don't Give a Darn."

"Who?" the officer asked again.

Roger smiled, "Yeah, Who's on first."

The chief was smiling too, "Yeah, Who's on first. I can see this is going to be interesting in more ways than one."

Roger said, "And the dog's name is…" and both men said in unison, "K9."

Roger added, "Looks like we are finally on the same page."

"What?"

"What's on second," Roger said, "and please, can we get on with this? I got through everything I think I need for the first investigation, but I want to come back tomorrow and do some more checking, especially in the area where Speedy thinks the old looking skulls came from."

"Sounds like a plan," Chief Bill Kenney said. "Tell me what you need to do to wrap this up for the day, and we will be outta here."

"Great," Roger said. "I'm out of Jack, and I need him."

"I told you to lighten up on that stuff for your own good."

Roger said, "I'll follow the doctor's orders."

The chief could not resist, "Who?"

Roger grimaced, "Yeah, that's the one." He shook his head and said to his tormenter. "What's the penalty for throwing your boss in the black swamp water?"

"Don't even think about it. Death by slow torture or worst."

"Thought so," Roger said. "You get those boxes over there," pointing with his finger, "and I'll get those tools still scattered about, and then we will be outta here for the day."

"Then what are we waiting for?"

The two men gathered up the items and placed them in the truck. Roger went to the dog now known as K9 and brought her to the truck. Bill said, "She goes in the back with the cargo. I'm not risking a repeat of this morning."

"Okay, okay, I'll put her in the back."

Roger lifted the young dog, sat her in the truck bed, tied her off, and whispered to her, "Don't take it personal. His bark is worse than his bite."

"What did you say?" the chief asked. "I didn't hear you."

Roger rolled his eyes, thought fast, and said, "Oh, I was thinking out loud. We need to stop at the office and give them an update. We need to have them barricade this road when someone is not here on site."

"That's good thinking. That's why I recommended you to myself for this job."

"More like made me an offer I couldn't refuse."

"Whatever. Let's concentrate on the important issue. A woman has died, and we want to find who done it."

"Agreed," Roger said. "Now hurry it up. Jack is calling my name, and he needs me."

More like you need him, thought the officer. *He got through the first day and really got a lot done. Maybe this will work out. It better. I don't have any more options. God help us.*

"Hey," Bill said. "I've got an idea. Let's stop at Fat Boy's BBQ and get a feast for two carryout. I'm buying too. You need to know about how the investigation is going, and I would like you to fill me in all that has happened to you. You know, the screw job they did to you at the college, and I really would like to know about your late wife and son. I think it would be good if you got some of that burden off your back."

Roger looked at his boss. "Fat Boy's is my favorite BBQ down here, of course it's the only one I've been to. You sure know how to get a guy's attention." He sighed. "Get the BBQ, and I'll tell you all about my work today. The rest is gonna be harder. It's still an open wound, but I think you're right. I need to talk about what happened." Roger looked at the Chief of Police and said, "You're a sly old fox. Bet you think if I drink less because of my problems, things will go a lot smoother for both of us."

Bill Kenney smiled, "Was I that transparent? I thought after all these years dealing with the public and criminals; I had a better poker face."

Now it was Roger's turn to smile. "I just know you too well, growing up together as boys and being second cousins on our mother's side helps me see your motivation."

"Busted," Bill Kenney said. "And you have to admit; I'm a lot cheaper than a shrink."

Roger nodded his head. "And you know the way to my heart, BBQ. Plus, I think you really like my dog. You know as well as I do, she'll get the rib bones when we're done with them."

Bill Kenney frowned, "She can do the cleanup, but I'm still not ready to forgive for her expunging all over my truck. That'll require some more time and effort on her part."

"Okay," Roger said. "I can live with that. Who knows? Maybe she will save you too."

Bill rolled his eyes. "Right, let's get that BBQ and continue this at your place."

"Sounds like a plan," Roger said.

And so they did.

Chapter 9

The BBQ from Fat Boys was excellent. They washed it down with beer from a 12-pack of Yuengling Lager they had gotten from Bill's refrigerator at his bungalow and the little dog, K9, enjoyed the leftovers including the rib bones. With tasty food in their stomachs along with three beers each, the men were in a pleasant mood. After supper, they moved the tools Roger had been using at the dig site from Bill's truck to Roger's. He would need them tomorrow.

Roger got a folding aluminum beach chair out for Bill to sit in and he then plopped down in the old overstuffed La-Z-Boy chair. White innards were sticking out from it in numerous places, but Roger could care less about that. It was his favorite spot in his man cave, actually his screened porch, attached to his old trailer.

Bill grabbed two more beers and popped them open. "Looks like I'm buying tonight."

"Yeah, looks like you are, Bill," Roger said. "Good old Pennsylvania beer. Remind me to thank all those Germans who settled the state for bringing their brewing skills with them."

Bill Kenney nodded in agreement, but he had another reason for the beer tonight. If Roger drank his usual hard liquor, he would be too plastered to give the information Bill wanted, and the beers should be enough to loosen his tongue and keep him going. From experience, he knew how to get the information he needed from people the easy way or through a little deception.

Bill began, "So tell me what you learned today."

"Buncha stuff, I told you a lot, but I'll review for you," said Roger. "I can't see this being anything but a murder probably by strangulation with the rope around her neck. I think she was raped and then posed in the grave in the peat bog by the killer. There're some sick puppies out there who enjoy toying with their victims, and this seems the case to me. The woman's body was in remarkable condition for someone buried, probably for a month, as I can best reason. She was naked and had a rose tattoo on her left ankle. I searched the immediate area around where she was and found nothing unusual. I'll look again tomorrow when I check out the lower area where Speedy said he thought the old bones came from." He stopped and took a big swig of beer. "Oh, I did find one more thing as I think I mentioned. Her one remaining hand was around her back, and it had duct tape on the wrist. This fell out of the hand as I uncovered her. I believe it could be the key to the whole case if we can figure what it is and who's it was."

He took a small plastic bag out of his pocket, pulled out the pin, and held it in his hand for Bill to see. Bill took the pin between his fingers. "Hmm, looks like an emblem or possibly a medal of some sort. Seems to have two reddish SS's on it. Kind of reminds me of someone's initials they would pin to a lapel. Steve Stinnett or maybe Sharon Smith or Sylvester Stallone? What do you think? Maybe SS as in Super Sport like on a Chevy muscle car?"

"Could be that or something else," said Roger. "Look on the back. Seems to be some kind of lettering or numbers. I can't make it out, but I think with some cleaning up and forensic work with a metal etching reagent, I can figure out what it says."

"I think you could be right about this being the key to finding the killer," said Bill.

Both men stopped and took long swigs of beer. Bill stood to his feet and said, "I think Archie Bunker was right. You can't own beer. You can only rent it."

Roger replied, "He was right about that. Bathrooms on the right. You can't miss it. Don't be like a college roommate I had. He had some serious drinking problems. He came in looped one night, made all kinds of noise as he stumbled around, and then in his confused state, pissed in my boots. I watched in disbelief as he did it. I knew he wasn't pleasant when he was that drunk, so I washed out the boots and left them in the shower. He got up all hungover the next morning and asked about the boots in the shower. I told him what he had done. He swore off for a week. Last I heard, he got fired from his latest job for drinking."

Bill looked at his friend, "Do you want to end up like that?"

Roger's face looked like a dose of salts had gone through him. He dropped his head but said nothing. Bill went on into the trailer, found the bathroom, relieved himself, and returned to the porch where he sat back down on the beach chair. He said, "Didn't know how bad I had to go. Think my eyes were floating."

Roger crawled out of the chair and stood unsteadily. "Think I better take care of business, too." He walked into the trailer and returned after a few minutes.

Roger said, "I hear what you say about my drinking, but right now, it's the only thing that eases the pain in my heart." He plopped down into the old recliner.

The two men said nothing for several minutes as they sipped on their beers. Roger sighed and said, "You know, I think I'll take that pin over to the library in Port St. John tomorrow. Maybe the people there can help me identify the pin."

"Good idea," said Bill. "See if Connie, the research lady, is working. She's good finding things. 'Me and her used to do some serious research after hours together after she got divorced from her second husband."

A short snort went from Roger's nose. "An old girlfriend? I should have known."

"Yeah," commented Bill. "She never could resist a uniform."

Roger made an ugly face. "You can spare me the details."

"Okay," Bill said, "but she's the 'go-to' person at the library. She knows her stuff."

Roger was pleased with the information. Bill had given him more than he wanted to know on Connie's abilities, and he had said "stuff," not the usual word for bull droppings Bill liked to use instead of stuff. Roger took another drink of beer and asked, "So, how do you think the Shaman fellow fits into this if at all?"

Bill rubbed his chin with the fingers of his right hand. "Can't say I know. I never had any dealings with him first-hand like lucky you, but I did have this one fellow, a man wanted by the feds, surrender to me. He crawled in from the marshes of the St. John River that border the west of Canaveral Flats all covered with mosquito bites and muck and literally begged me to save him, take him in. Never saw a man so scared and wanting to go to jail. He was practically babbling incoherently when he found me. When I got him handcuffed and calmed down, he told me this crazy tale about encountering some wild man out in the swamp. I figured he had run into the Shaman and it hadn't gone well for the fugitive. But it may not have been the Shaman. There's some other characters livin' out in that swamp that like their privacy and want nothing to do with civilization." He stopped and took a drink of beer. "My advice is to be on the alert for the unusual when you're at the crime scene."

Even with the beer buzz, Roger knew he would remember this. He nodded and said, "I think I'd like to meet this Shaman guy again. I have some questions I want to ask him, even if his answers are riddles like his statement to me earlier today."

"Just be careful," Bill said. "Don't need my second-in-command, friend, and only help on this case to be hurt. Know what I mean?"

"I do," Roger replied.

The two men sat in quiet. It was getting dark, and the distant streetlight cast a dim light on where they were. A few stars were visible. Both men sipped at their beers. It seemed neither wished to be the one to bring up the elephant in the room, but Bill broke the silence. "So tell me in your own words without spin, what happened at the college and with your wife and son that drove you down here."

Chapter 10

Roger said nothing for a moment, sighed, and slowly began. "Guess you are cheaper than talking with a head-shrink and you're the closest thing I have to a confidant in this world. The one that I had died and that's what we need to be talking about." He paused for a moment. "And there's another benefit talking with you."

"What's that?" asked Bill.

"Beer," said Roger. "You brought the beer and will keep them coming as long as I keep talking, right?"

Bill could see that his plan was exposed, so he saw no point in denying it. He nodded.

A coy smile came to Roger's face. He'd been down the pike a few times too. "Hope you got money for more beer," he said. "This may take a while."

Bill nodded again and said, "Okay, Mr. Detective, now you got that out in the open, can we begin?"

"Certainly," Roger said. He finished his beer, rose unsteadily, and got another one from the cooler. He sat down, popped the top, and took a big swig. "Aw, good Pennsylvania beer, even if it does come from Tampa." He looked at Bill for a reaction.

"Tampa?" Bill said. "Thought their brewery was in Pottstown, PA."

"Their original one was up there, but they recently bought out the old Schlitz plant in Tampa, and now they have two breweries to keep up with the demand," Roger answered.

"Did not know that," Bill said.

"Yup, they nearly were broke and bankrupt a decade ago. All American comeback success story."

Bill said, "Not sure what this has to do with your story, other than you like the beer I am buying and want to keep it coming."

Roger said, "I was getting to that before I was so rudely interrupted." He stopped for effect. "A few years ago when they were having difficulties, they hired a consultant to help them with their problem. After some studies, he got back with them and astonished them with his findings. He said they needed to raise their prices. He told them they had a great product, but were selling it at too cheap a price. People saw it with the cheap beers and passed it by for a higher-priced beer they assumed was better. They had little choice but to follow his advice even though some on the board thought it madness, but they did. Sales slowly rebounded, and then took off, and now they have the recently added brewery in Tampa. Got it?"

Bill said, "Guessed I missed it. What are you trying to say?"

Roger rolled his eyes. "I should have known I would have to spell it out for a dumb hillbilly."

"And don't forget that dumb hillbilly is also your boss and friend keeping you out of the drunk tank."

Roger grimaced at that. "Okay, I gotcha. What they learned at the brewery was this; when you have a problem, get help. That's why I decided to cooperate with you."

Bill nodded that he understood and both men took another swig of their Yuengling beer.

Roger said, "I want to go back a little further to when we were boys and then come forward to the present. That okay with you?"

"It is if it's not an excuse to draw this out and for me to buy more beer," Bill answered.

Roger faked surprise. "Why I'm shocked. Now, you know me better than that, ole buddy."

Bill gave a fake smile back. "Get on with it."

Roger turned the beer up and drank heartily. "Oh, all right. You know how it was growing up in the little town of Fort Ashby, West Virginia? Everybody knew each other."

"Yup," Bill said. "About like here. Everyone knows everyone and all their business, good, bad, or indifferent."

"That's how it was for us growing up as neighbors. I knew you as a kid as well as I knew the back of my hand from all the time we spent together whether it was bike riding, playing together, practicing our Little League baseball skills, or swimming in Patterson Creek."

"Yeah, most of the time it was skinny dippin,'" Bill said. "Remember that time those girls from Cumberland who had the summer cottage on the crick thought it would be a hoot to steal our clothes, which they did."

"How could I forget that?" Roger said. "I still remember the look on their faces as they ran down the dirt road with our clothes and us naked as jaybirds in hot pursuit. When we got near to them, they threw our clothes over a barbed wire fence into the cow pasture, let out a holler that would raise the dead, and ran twice as fast. Once we retrieved our clothes, we let them getaway. We had what we wanted and needed."

"I remember. Slipping through a barbed wire fence naked was not my idea of a fun time. Bet they're still talking about it to this day," Bill said.

A big smile came to Roger's face. "They are. Let you in on a little secret. One of those girls became my wife."

"No way," Bill exclaimed.

Roger nodded. "I met my wife at a football event before a game at a Christian Athletics Association tailgate forum at the college where I was a professor. She was big into that stuff at the time, and I was there for the free food, and you know me, the atheist I was back then, maybe to stir the pot a little, but not enough to get me thrown out and miss on the free food."

Bill laughed. "You haven't changed. Free food, free beer, I'll find you there."

"True. Kay was friendly. We hit it off, but she liked to blew me away when she asked me if I remembered chasing three girls who had taken our clothes when they caught us skinny dippin'. I stood there with my mouth wide open and my jaw dragging the ground. You could have knocked me over with a feather after she looked me over from head to toe and said with a big grin on her face, 'I thought you looked familiar.' I didn't know it at the time, but she was to see me naked a whole bunch later," he said and coyly added,

66

"And me her. That's how I met my wife, but I'm getting ahead of myself in this story."

The two men finished off their beers. "That's a funny story, and I guess you will get around to the rest of it eventually."

"I will," Roger said, "but I wanted to go back a bit to something that had stuck with me all these years from when we were little and growing up. You remember going to the little yellow brick church at the end of the road?"

"How could I forget?" Bill said. "Everybody went. I had a lot of fun there with the other kids and learned some things too."

"And free food," Roger added.

"And free food," Bill echoed. "Somehow, I knew free food would come up."

Roger laughed. "You remember the preacher, Mr. O'Reilly?"

"How could I forget him?" Bill answered. "Ex-Marine with a crew cut, tough as nails, and gentle as a lamb, unless you got him mad which wasn't often."

"That's the guy. He was all the time telling us about the 'straight and narrow way,' and we were always testing him with questions to see what he believed and if we could catch him with a gotcha question."

"He had to have the patience of Job when dealing with us young hellions."

Roger nodded in agreement. "He did. A lot of his stories and influence stuck with me over the years, even when, as a teenager, I walked away from church. Figured I didn't need it and it didn't make sense with some of the stuff I was taught in high school and college."

It was quiet for a moment. Bill spoke, "After Mom died, and I went to live with Dad here in Florida, my church days were over, but yeah, every now and then, I remember what Mr. O'Reilly said and as I age, it makes more sense."

"That's a big 10-4, good buddy," Roger replied.

"Hey, I want to hear the rest of your story as we drink **my** beer," Bill said. "How about you get on with it?"

Roger took a long drag on the beer, smacked his lips, and said, "Yup, you have some quality tastes in beer, my friend and boss. Let's see. Where was I? Oh yeah, meeting my wife. You're not gonna believe this, but it goes something like this. It was a cool and crisp fall day on the campus of Western Maryland University. Little did I know how by my being there for that event, how much my life was goin' to change."

Chapter 11

Roger began again, "It took me a little while to get over my em-bare-ass-ment after she had revealed the naked truth she knew about me. I laughed it off best I could. She said the girls sure thought it was funny, especially after they threw our clothes over a barbed wire fence onto some cows. Fortunately, our clothes landed on the backs of the cows, so we only had to chase them a short time, as you well remember."

Bill nodded, "Wish I could forget. It wasn't somethin' I would recommend not chasing cows while naked in a pasture with lots of fresh pies to step and slide in."

"How right you are, my drunken friend," Roger said. "Anyway, back to the day many years later, when I met my wife, Kay. We hit it off, and she invited me to sit with her group during the game. It sounded good to me, and so I did. It was somewhat different than the usual times I'd had at football games. This group did not drink or smoke whatever and nothing but wholesome language came out of their mouths even when the referees blew a call against the home team. It was somewhat refreshing for a change. I didn't even pull out the flask I had in my hip pocket. I knew they knew I had it, but no one made a big deal out of it."

Roger continued, "It was a great game, back and forth all four quarters, until the last play of the game on a broken play with our team, the Hilltoppers, down by five points, one of the players, can't remember his position, ran 50 yards and we won the game. Everyone was all happy, and everyone was hugging everyone. I got lots of hugs from the group there, but especially from Kay. As the excitement finally wore off and the noise around us died off, I got bold and asked her if she could and would like to have dinner with me after the game. To my surprise, she said yes, so we went over to Penn Alps Restaurant in Grantsville, Maryland and had a tasty meal. Afterward, we walked over to the Artisan Village and then to the old stone Casselman Bridge that the original path of National Road went on. Lots of history in that little wide spot. The old Indian named Nemacolin has a trail along there as did General Braddock of French & Indian War fame, and as I mentioned, the old National Road and US 40 and I 68 all passed by this place in the mountain valley. The fall colors were beautiful that evening which added to the romance of our first date."

Bill took a swig from his beer. "Guess you have a point in all this, or has the beer got your mouth goin' like a runaway truck down a mountain?"

Roger ignored the question. "I asked her for her phone number, and she gave to me but said these words, 'We had a good time today and I would like to see you again, but I know of your reputation with women so the first time you try anything funny, it will be your last time with me.'"

"Bet that got your attention," Bill said.

"It did. I wasn't used to being talked to so bluntly," Roger said, "but her honesty and feistiness was a welcome change from most of the gals I'd had relationships with. So I said okay, and that's when the best times and the worst times of my life began."

Bill said, "It was the best of times. It was the worst of times."

Roger nodded and took a big swig of beer. "Yup, like in the Charles Dickens novel, *Tale of Two Cities*."

There was silence between the two men. The little dog, K9, whimpered in her sleep. Bill spoke, "Now you have me curious. Are you going to continue this story?"

Roger took in a deep breath and let it out. "It's kinda hard to talk about it even today, but I think I need to tell you the rest. I've been holding it all in for so long," he lamented.

Chapter 12

"Well, as I said, we hit it off from the start. I was seeing her at least once a week for about five months and enjoying every minute of it, and there was no hanky panky like there had been with the numerous other girls," Roger said. "I came to the conclusion quickly she was my intellectual equal and not merely another pretty face on a great body. She challenged me in ways I'd never been challenged before."

"Yeah, I'm sure. The no-sex thing," Bill said, "must have been tough for an old horndog like you."

"Not as tough as you or I would have thought," Roger answered. "You see, I was beginning to love her, even with our differences. She told me upfront about her Christian faith and how her mother had advised her not to become too close to me, unequally yoked she called it, but Kay felt she could exit our relationship if it got to be a problem. And she got me to thinking, really thinking again — something I hadn't done in a long time. As I look back on it, I can see how she had been leading me along to this point. I'd been regurgitating what I'd been taught without questioning it, not asking if it could pass the truth test. I remember her saying, 'The problem is not uneducated people. We have plenty of those. The problem is they're just educated enough to swallow and believe what they're taught, but not educated enough to question what they're taught.' I can still remember when she said that. It went through me like a dose of salts. It was like one of those eureka moments for me. The more I thought about it, the more I knew she was right. She wanted me to think and search for truth and fact which I did, and I encourage everyone to do this. Look at both sides and then make up your mind based on evidence, not someone's opinion they've claimed was the truth."

Bill took a drink, swallowed, and then spoke. "That's some pretty heavy-duty industrial strength wisdom. I can see where you get your inquiring mind."

"She was a tremendous influence on me," Roger said. "She was full of smarts and zingers which she threw out regularly like, 'Common sense doesn't come with a degree, professor,' and on the same line, 'It's a flower that doesn't grow in everyone's garden.'"

"I've met many people like she was describing," Bill said. "They think they are so smart and can barely tie their own shoes, totally devoid of horse sense. We get a lot of Yankees coming down here that think we're a bunch of hayseeds and they can talk down to us like we were yahoos. They're usually the ones we get the calls on for help. Anything from sunburned to a crisp, like a boiled lobster, and needin' to know where the hospital is, or chomped on by a gator or cottonmouth, drowned in a riptide, or stuck in sugar sand. If I had a nickel for every one of them I had to help or rescue, why, I'd been a rich man."

"I know the type," Roger said. "Unfortunately, there's a smidgen of them everywhere."

Bill nodded, "I'm beginning to get the picture. Go on. Tell me more."

"After five months of dating and seeing no one but each other, I went on a two week trip to Europe doing some archaeologist's fieldwork, you know, looking at old bones and bodies. Some of it was in France, and I picked up a bottle of wine to take home. It was recommended to me by one of the locals in the group. We were near Spain, and it turned out the wine was more like sherry and had an alcohol content of nearly 20%, though I did not find this out till much later. That part of the label was rubbed on by something in my suitcase on the trip home. Kay was happy to see me when I arrived home. She made me a special dinner, and we celebrated with the wine. I did not know she had a weakness for French wine. We finished off the whole bottle, one thing led to another, and we woke up the next morning naked in her bed."

Roger went on, "We had a long talk that morning. I told her I was surprised it happened, but not unhappy about it. She told me about her weakness for wine and not to expect any more nights like we had just had unless we were husband and wife. I knew she meant it, and it never happened again. Two months later, she told me she was pregnant. She didn't know what to do and was very upset, but I knew what I wanted and needed to do. I asked her if she would give me the honor of her hand in marriage. I knew we had our differences, but I wanted her, and I wanted the child to have a proper mommy and daddy. She said, 'Yes,' but her mother was not too happy about us not having the same faith. Her dad took it better. He liked me and pulled me aside later. With a wink in his eye, he said, 'Don't think you're the first young couple in the history of the world to let your hormones get the best of you.' I was surprised by his reaction. It was, later on, I found out there were only five months between her father and mother's wedding and the birth of Kay's older brother. They'd been married forty years at the time of my proposal to Kay."

"True to her wishes, we did not have relations again till our wedding night, a month later, and what a night it was. Don't expect any more details. What goes on between lovers like we were, does not need to be talked or written about. Besides, your imagination as to what went on is probably wilder."

Bill laughed, "Yeah, I do have a vivid imagination. Don't betray the trust she had in you even now."

"I'll not," Roger said. "Six months later, little Robert, who we called Bobby, was born, seven pounds, thirteen ounces. I was a blessed man. It was a great two years of marriage we had together, well mostly." He stopped. "That morning, she put Bobby in his car seat in her little two-seat sports car. I told her I wanted her to buy something bigger, but she loved her little sports car and wouldn't do it. Less than two miles from the house, doing 55 mph, she hit a big buck. The deer took out the windshield, fell on them and then the car hit a sycamore tree. If the blunt force from the deer didn't kill them, the crash into the tree did. And before she left, she told me she was pregnant again. You talk about getting blindsided."

The two men were quiet for a moment. "I'm sorry," Bill said. "I'd heard a little bit about what happened, but not all this. I can see why you'd drink."

Roger began again, "I had a cousin who sold insurance. He convinced us to buy some life insurance on both of us. You never know what could happen, he said. I expected it would be me gone instead of her if anyone died. At our young age, it was cheap, so we got a big dollar policy, and that's what I've been livin' on. I won't have to worry about money for a long time."

"There's more I need to tell you for you to have the big picture. As I said, it was the best of times. It was the worst of times. The first year had its up and downs. We both thought about throwing in the towel several times, me mainly. It was tough on her balancing a job, a new baby, a home, and me. No wonder she was moody at times. One day her mother showed up and offered to babysit and give us the evening together. Guess she could see the wear and tear life was having on us. Kay wanted burgers, fries and a Frosty at Wendy's, so that's where we went. An old girlfriend of mine was there. I introduced her to my wife, and we dined together. I could tell my wife was a little suspicious of her at first, but after a few minutes, they were talking like old friends. Guess I must be a good judge of women."

Bill was taking a sip of beer at that moment and nearly snorted it out his nose. He coughed loudly. Roger said, "Okay, no comments from the cheap seats. Anyway, Kay went to the bathroom, and I got to talk with the old girlfriend for a couple of minutes. The only thing I remember of that conversation was this bit of advice that fell from her lips. I told her, 'That woman drives me crazy sometimes.' And she replied, 'We all do.' It was right then, and there I decided I was going to do everything I could to make this marriage work. Things got better afterward, and the rest of the time we were married was like a bowl of cherries. There still were some pits to deal with, but I would not have traded the time with them for all the gold in the world."

"I'll have to remember that," Bill said. "Sounds like a gal I'd like to meet."

"You never know," Roger said. "Last I heard about her by the grapevine; she took a job at the University of Central Florida over Orlando way. Anyway, as I said, it was the best of times. It was the worst of times. She opened my eyes to so much, and that got me in trouble on campus. Before, I had been one of the guys who went along with the crowd and thought as they did. Turns out the crowd only loves you when you agree with them. She questioned what she'd been taught in church and public education. She said it grounded her in her faith, and many times when I had questions, she explained it for me. Evolution was something she thought was foolish. By evolution, I mean the theory of nothing to something to goo to the zoo to you and millions and millions of years. It was taught as fact, but did not stand up to serious scientific scrutiny."

"You have me curious," Bill said. "I hear and see it all over the place just as you say. How is it not scientific?"

"Now that's a heavy-duty question you're asking a man with a high blood-alcohol content," Roger answered, "but I will try to give you the best response my fuzzy brain can under the circumstances."

Bill laughed and said, "Drunks can solve all the problems in the world when under the influence, but the problem is, they can never remember what the solutions are the next morning."

"How right you are," Roger said. "For something to be a scientific fact, it must pass the two requirements of the scientific method. It must be repeatable and observable. Now tell me, can you recreate and observe the beginning of the earth and universe and everything living in it?"

Bill rubbed his chin as he thought on this question. "No, don't think you can. I don't think even a sober person could disagree with that. Why, you'd have to be God to do that."

"Exactly," Roger replied. "You're beginning to sound like my late wife. We still argued over how old the earth was, millions and millions of years or somewhere between six thousand and eight thousand years as she believed. Not sure what I believed or if it made any difference, but I can't see how nothing ever made something."

"Did you ask her who made God?" Bill asked.

"That sounds like a question we would have thrown at Mr. O'Reilly," Roger said. "She said God was the uncreated Creator. I didn't understand her point until she showed me using surveying."

"Surveying? Now you lost me," Bill said.

"I was a little lost at first too, but she explained it simply." Roger continued, "In surveying, you have to start with a known point. It all makes sense when you consider this: 'In the beginning, God created the heavens and the earth.'"

"Think I've heard it somewhere before," Bill said.

"Yup, God never explains His existence. I don't think we would understand. He tells us He is and what He did. He lets us figure out the rest, and sometimes the figuring often is full of holes."

"How so?" Bill asked.

"Million-year-old dinosaur bones with blood and soft tissue in them that's only known to last six thousand years. Rocks that came out of a volcano in 1853 dated by one Ivy League school as 100 million years old and by another as 200 million years old, or fish like the Coelacanth said to be extinct for 70 million years turning up very much alive. The book of Genesis in the Bible says as kinds begat like kinds, but evolution books say one kind becomes another. One we can observe and one we can't, so tell me which is science-based and which is faith-based? There're many others, but I won't bore you with more facts. You can do what I did, Mr. Inquiring Mind. Look them up and see for yourself," Roger said.

Bill looked at Roger very seriously.

"Why are you looking at me that way?" Roger asked.

Bill cleared his alcohol tainted throat. "I got one question for you. A serious question for you and I hope you will answer it. From what you have told me, your wife seems to have convinced you that her beliefs were true. So, why haven't you done this 'born again' thing, you know, come to Jesus?"

Roger let out a deep breath, took another drink of beer, and said, "You ask a hard question, and I think I want to give you an answer. Yes, she did have me thinking seriously about doing exactly that, but then this God who I was beginning to think was took everything I held dear away from me." A tear rolled down Roger's face. "So I guess I'm mad at a God I'm not even sure exists for what He's done to me. Now, do you see why I drink?"

The two men sat silently as more tears rolled down Roger's face. After a moment, Bill spoke, "I understand you a whole lot better. It takes a big man to get a burden like that off his back."

"Then, let me completely unload," Roger said. "The new inquiring me soon lost his welcome at the campus. I was teaching my students to think critically and inquire with hard questions, and the other professors didn't like to be challenged. It was so much easier to spew out what was fashionable, the truth at the moment, some call it 'politically correct' and all. I was up for tenure, and word came back to me the big wheels in the faculty and administration were not going to give it to me. Funny, how real free-thinking was no longer welcome on a university campus. Only correct thinking was permitted, and all else would be punished. I always thought you should treat people kindly, even those you disagreed with, but they showed they had other ideas. How else are people goin' to work together and learn from each other?

"Anyway, I had a few aces up my sleeve, and I used them. I had a friend at the local paper that ran a story about how they were trying to railroad me out. They made mention of all the forensic work I'd done for the police - local, state, and federal, and asked how a man of my caliber would be denied tenure. Alumni in positions of power and also those whose deep pockets helping fund the school began to put heat on the administration. Still, they held out."

"Then my wife and son were killed, and it knocked out the fight out of me. After the funeral, the head of the school offered me this deal. They would give me tenure and a sum of money if I would quietly go away and not return to the school. It was a very unusual and special deal. It wasn't the victory I wanted, but I was tired of fightin', and it was time to move on so I took it and here I am today with a little dog named K9, a boss who needs my help finding a dead woman's killer and a drinking problem. That sums it up. Now, are you happy you've heard the complete story?"

Bill took a drink from his beer. He tipped it up to get the last of it and threw the can into the growing pile in the trash can. He looked at Roger and smiled, "There's a lot more to you than what meets the eye, Roger Pyles, a truckload more. It takes a big man to open up like that. I understand you much more. You've gotten this far. You'll work your way to wherever you're going as soon as you figure where that is."

Roger said, "I hope you're right, but then, you are the boss."

"That I am and tomorrow's another day, and it'll be here soon whether we've slept or not, so without further ado, I'm staggering home. Don't forget to stop over at the library and ask my lady friend about the pin before you go to the Windover site, ole buddy. And thanks for sharing that with me. Not every day, someone trusts a cop to unburden themselves on."

Bill was rubber-legged as he left. Roger could follow him with his eyes as Bill headed for the road. He nearly stumbled over a coquina rock that Roger had in his yard as a decoration, but he recovered before damage was done.

The little dog adjusted herself on the bed Roger had bought at the shelter. "You know dog, this may work out, but I ain't gonna hold my breath." He did feel better after telling someone about his problems, but he still didn't feel right. *Maybe something stronger would help.* He pulled the flask of bourbon from his pocket and took a drink. *Yup, wonder what tomorrow will bring?*

Chapter 13

Those who want to live, let them fight, and those who do not want to fight in this world of eternal struggle do not deserve to live. Adolf Hitler

The old man sat on the bar sipping a Beck's beer. It was the best he could get today. It was hard to find a good German or Belgian beer in Florida even when you own the bar, or for that matter, the whole establishment commonly called Stiltsville. He loved all the beers the DuPont Brewery of Tourpes, Belgium produced especially the Posca Rustica gruit. What a treasure they were when he could find them. Though the beers brewed in Belgium, the family who ran and owned the brewery were of good German stock going back for many centuries. The beer reminded him of the grand old days back home before and during the war, when the Reich was moving to create an empire to last one thousand years. Things had not gone according to the Fuhrer's plans he had outlined in Mein Kampf, but the struggle continued. The words: loyalty, honor, and duty, even to death rang in his head. How many times had he heard them during the war? He believed them then, and he still did, but the years were catching up with him. Would the dream of a Fourth Reich arising from the ashes ever happen? It did not look like it would occur in his lifetime, but the dream among the believers did not die easily — loyalty, honor, and duty, even to death.

He was tired. When he looked in the mirror, he saw Father Time or was it just him? Either way, he knew his years on planet Earth were growing short. Loyalty, honor, and duty, even to death.

He took a long sip on his beer. The article on page two of the local paper, *Florida Today,* troubled him. The body of another young girl had been found near the Kennedy Space Center. He looked through the open-air hut which was called a chickee by the

79

local Seminole builders who had constructed it. It gave the place a tropical feel and seemed to put the patrons at ease in his establishment. He could see the space center's tall and massive Vehicle Assembly Building and several launch pads on the horizon about twelve miles away. Nothing blocked his view over the Indian River Lagoon but a few distant trees. He wondered if the man he called Valentino had been busy again. How he hated cleaning up after him, but the orders from years ago had been to assist and protect those who had escaped the Allies' traps. But, he was tired. And Valentino was an asset too valuable to lose. He knew it, and Valentino knew it. Valentino did what he pleased. Therein lies the problem. Valentino's actions could draw attention to the whole secret operation. There had already been mistakes made, and a person in the public eye like Valentino could bring unwanted scrutiny upon their covert operation. Loyalty, honor, and duty.

With the help of sympathizers and people who could be bought, he had obtained false papers and a passport to bring him to Miami in the confusion in Europe after the war. He had gold and millions of counterfeit dollars the Reich had printed, so good that they fooled even the experts. It was in Miami he first conceived the idea of building his own Stiltsville someplace else in Florida after visiting the compound called Quarterdeck Club which was surrounded by Biscayne Bay. What a place. It stood on the barely submerged sand flats. Liquor flowed freely among the rich and famous. Gambling was available as were beautiful women who came at a price. It had the added advantage of being in a place where you could see a boat coming from miles away. No one, especially Johnny Lawman, could sneak up on the watering hole. Lawyers, politicians, bankers, judges, and the well-connected visited to drink, relax, and kickback. And he had found the ideal spot for his establishment two hundred miles north in the Indian River Lagoon between Titusville and Cocoa in a rapidly developing area.

Corrupt officials who will look the other way are everywhere, and this place was no exception. In six months, the first part of Stiltsville was up and running as he had envisioned. With the combination of liquor, gambling, loose women, and a no-tell, look the other way atmosphere, his establishment became more prominent and the place to go after hours, making it very profitable. Money went to buy the silence of local law enforcement and also back to the group which had helped him elude the International Military Tribunal at Nuremberg. For that, he would be eternally grateful — loyalty, honor, and duty unto death for the cause.

Yes, he was tired. How much longer could he keep up this charade, this façade of who he was and what was going on below the surface? It had been almost four decades. There should be more to show for their effort, or was the big plan to keep it all quiet until they could surprise and astonish the world as they quickly retook power? He wondered and drank a long draw on the can of Becks. How he wished he had a gruit beer instead. He hoped Valentino had nothing to do with this woman's death, but if he was a betting man, and he was, he would bet Valentino was involved. He had been careful and lucky so far for the most part, and he, the old man Heyrich, had taken care of the loose ends of Valentino's lusts before, but he was getting very tired of it. Valentino could become a liability instead of an asset and bring the whole plan crashing down if his deeds ever saw the light of day. Heyrich could see Valentino was walking the razor's edge even if Valentino didn't want to see it. Whatever orders reached him, he would cleanse the problem. Loyalty, honor, and duty unto death for the cause no matter whose death it was.

Chapter 14

There's always going to be the circumstances you can't plan for. There's always the unexpected relevance and the serendipity. Jason Silva

The next morning, Roger awake to doggy kisses on his face. "Dog, what do you want?" he barked at her as she danced around the screened porch. His own full bladder answered the question. He opened the screen door and let the dog out. She quickly squatted and urinated. Roger unzipped his fly and did the same. *Don't feel like home till you pissed in your own front yard. Hope the neighbors done went to work.*

"Now don't you run away or the dog catcher will get you," Roger said. He found the rope he had used earlier and tied it to the dog's collar. "Got to get you a proper chain and some real dog food. Maybe that will keep your guts from going into overdrive and revolution today. Don't need a repeat performance."

Roger walked K9 over to his truck, opened the door, and said. "Get in, dog. We have to get you some food over at the Winn Dixie, and I think I'll have breakfast at that Umpa's place next door. Sound like a plan? Maybe they'll make me a sandwich for my lunch. Wonder if they have fried bologna? Bet you would like one too."

The little dog seemed to understand and jumped into the truck. Roger started it up and was soon passing Miller's Store on the washboard road called Canaveral Flats Boulevard. He took a left on US 1, drove for a mile, and took another left at the Winn Dixie Plaza. He found a parking spot near the grocery store, but none in front of Umpa's which looked crowded inside. Roger knew a crowd was a good sign for comfort food, and after the beer bender last night, he needed something more substantial than liquid to stick to his innards. "You stay right here," he said to K9. "I'll be right back with some chow for you, okay?"

The dog laid down on the seat as Roger tied the rope to the steering wheel. "I won't be long, and see, I'm leaving the windows down so you won't overheat."

Roger walked to the automatic front door that opened for him. He grabbed a shopping cart and started toward the pet section. It shook as one wheel wobbled back and forth. "Figures," Roger grumbled to himself, "I'd get one with a bum wheel."

He found what he wanted in the pet section, got it, went to check out, paid, and walked to the truck carrying the supplies. "Hey, little doggy, look what I have for you? Breakfast and dinner. Hope you like the store brand."

K9 wagged her tail as Roger changed out the chain for the rope which the dog had chewed about halfway through. Roger looked at the rope. "K9, I don't know if you were bored and needed a chewy thing or you were trying to escape. Hope it was the former. Just the same, don't think about jumping out the window and taking off for God only knows where. Not a good idea. You'd get run over and end up with four broken legs. And then you'd come running to me for help. Let's you and me give this arrangement a chance. I think we'd make a good team." K9 gave a doggy smile and continued to wag her tail.

"Looks like I forgot to get you a bowl. Hope you don't mind eating off the floor till I get you one." Roger poured a large amount on the rubber floor mats. "There you go. I'll be right back after I have my breakfast, okay?"

An elderly lady walked up to the car parked next to him. Roger was somewhat embarrassed when she caught him talking to the dog. She smiled and said, "Young man, it's okay to talk to your pet. Since my Charlie died a decade ago, I haven't had anyone to talk to so my little Pomeroy has been my sounding board. It sure makes me feel better. My dog seems to enjoy the additional attention."

"Well, thank you for that bit of advice, ma'am," Roger said. "I lost my wife two years ago, and it's been a rough and lonely time since her passing."

"I know, young man," she said. "I felt like part of me died when I lost my husband. It's a little easier as time goes by, but I don't think I'll ever get over it, nor do I want to. Forty years of marriage gives you lots of memories. What's your name, young man?"

"Roger Pyles."

"Well, Roger Pyles," she said, "my name's Betsy Winn."

"Please to meet you, ma'am." Roger asked, "Is it 'Winn' as in Winn Dixie?"

"It is, though I could only wish it was the 'Winn,' as in the owners of Winn Dixie, but that's someone else." She smiled. "Do you live local?"

"Yes, I do," Roger said. "Over in Canaveral Flats. I'm helping out with the investigation of the body they found in the new Windover housing development."

"Oh, I saw an article about that in the local paper, *Florida Today*," she said.

Roger said, "Looks like bad news travels fast."

"It does," Betsy Winn said. "Faster than horses' hooves. I better let you go, young man. I'm sure you have better things to do than prattle on with an old lady."

"Oh, no problem, ma'am," Roger said. "It's good to talk to another human. I've been a kind of a recluse since my wife passed."

She looked at Roger with sympathy. "I'll pray for you, Roger Pyles."

"Thank you, ma'am," Roger said. "Say, you know anything about Umpa's? I never have been in it, and was wondering how the food was?"

"Do I know about Umpa's? Why, as a matter of fact, I do," she said. "Since the passing of my husband, I've been the sole owner and my daughter, Marsha, is running the restaurant for me. Great American-style breakfast and lunch, closes at two P.M. Open every day except Wednesday."

"Thank you very much for that information, ma'am," Roger said. "I'm sure it'll be great."

"If it ain't, you make sure I hear about it, okay?"

"Will do," Roger said. "I'm sure it'll be fine."

She nodded, "Good to talk with you, young man. I'll be praying for you."

"Thank you," Roger said. "I'll take all the help I can get. Let me help you with your bags."

"Would you do that for an old lady? I'd appreciate it greatly."

Roger helped her with the supermarket buggy full of bags. He said, "You've enough here to feed an army."

She smiled. "Marsha and her two boys, Brian and Dayton, my grandsons, live with me. Their no good father walked out on them about five years ago, and they've been living with me ever since. Enough of me rattling on. You better feed your stomach before it eats your backbone."

"That sounds like something they would say up in the hills of West Virginia where I come from," Roger said.

"Close, but no cigar," she said. "We hail from the other Virginia down near Galax along the New River, but still in those beautiful mountains. Seems like 'bout everyone here is from someplace up north. Like them all, except for some of those damned know-it-alls, everything's better up north New York Yankees bums." She stopped. "Young man, I want you to get in there and have some breakfast or some old lady will talk your leg off and tell you how she really feels." She smiled.

Roger smiled too. "I will, ma'am. It was a pleasure to talk to you. Have a great day."

"You, too, young man," she said. "And I'll be praying for you."

Roger nodded his head, went to the door of the restaurant, and walked in. The décor was nothing special: a few mismatched knick knacks and several pictures with Florida scenes decorated the interior. A young woman about 35 years old with strawberry blond hair and wire-rim glasses entered the room from what Roger could tell was the kitchen. She wore jeans and a tee-shirt with a large Umpa's Restaurant logo on the front along with Marsha on her name tag. The cooking food aroma followed her. "Howdy," she said. "Welcome to Umpa's where you are a stranger only once. Do you need a menu or would you like our special of the day?"

She pointed to a whiteboard. It read, "Scrambled eggs, two strips bacon, burnt toast, home fries, coffee -$3.50."

"Looks good, except for the burnt toast," Roger replied.

"Burnt toast?" The surprised look on her face turned to a scowl. "Bill's been up to his tricks again. I'd call the law on him if he wasn't the law already."

"Would that be possibly Bill Kenney of the Canaveral Flats Police Department?" Roger asked.

"That's him," she said. "The one and only. Also the one and only Canaveral Flats flat foot. He can be a real joker and cut up when he wants to be. Thinks being a cop gives him some special privileges and some discretion. Next time he's in here, I'll make sure he gets burnt toast. It will serve him right." She stopped, and Roger could tell from the look on her face that she thought she had said too much. "Is he perhaps a friend of yours?"

"Yeah, he's a friend of mine," Roger said, "and he's also my half-fast boss."

"Sounds like Bill," she said. "Say, did you say he was your boss? Didn't know Canaveral Flats had money for a second cop."

"I don't think they do, but that's a long story," Roger said. "I got shanghaied into helping him with the investigation of a girl's death here in town."

"I see," she said. "Why don't you take a spot anywhere and I'll have the cook whip up another special, minus the burnt toast, for you. Sound good? And do you want decaf or regular coffee?"

"I do," Roger said. "Regular and make my coffee strong and black."

"I thought you'd want it that way," she said. "Coming up in a shake of a lamb's tail."

Roger took a seat in a booth. As he sat down, the back swayed and pushed slightly against the back of a man who was reading the local newspaper in the next booth. The man, who appeared to be in his late sixties turned around. "Sorry," Roger said. "The booth's back seems to be broken. Sorry."

The man nodded. "It's quite alright," he said and went back to reading his newspaper. Roger noted a slight accent, German maybe, but not French or Spanish, perhaps one from Eastern Europe.

Marsha appeared at Roger's table with a pot of coffee in one hand and a cup in the other. She set the cup down and poured the dark liquid in. "There you go. Cook said your special would be out in a flash. You missed the early morning crowd. It was a madhouse in here earlier. Most of them left just before you came in. We were short-handed and busier than a one-armed paper hanger, but now we have a little breathing room until the lunch crowd comes in and we do it all over again."

"That is busy," Roger said. "That's another expression I haven't heard in years, busier than a one-armed paper hanger."

"I picked it up from my mom along with some other interesting utterings, some under my breath," she said.

"And your mother's name is Betsy Winn."

"How do you know that?" she asked.

Roger said, "I met her in the parking lot. Nice lady. I think she told me your whole life history."

Marsha grimaced. "That sounds like my momma. A heart of gold and a tongue that never stops wagging. Gotta love 'er. Sometimes she drives me nuts, but Lord only knows where I'd be if it wasn't for her."

Roger nodded. "She told me about the bad luck you had with your husband."

Marsha sighed. "That's my momma. I fuss at her about telling so much, but it's like arguing with a rock. You turn blue in the face, and the rock keeps on doing what a rock does. Say, has anyone ever told you that you remind them of Sam Elliott?"

"Would you believe me if I told you, you were the first one?" he asked.

"No, I wouldn't," she said.

"How about the second?"

They both laughed. At that time, the doors to the kitchen swung open, and a portly black woman wearing an apron which covered her street clothes appeared carrying the special Roger had ordered. She walked the few steps to the table and sat it down in front of Roger. It looked and smelled delicious. "Here you go, sir," she said. "Enjoy."

"Thank you," he said, "Miss…?"

"Cathy," the cook said. "Sometimes they call Cat and sometimes it's Big Black Cat and even BBC for short," She smiled and laughed. "You may have heard of me."

"Well, thank you, Miss Cat," he said. "I do believe I have heard of the BBC."

She smiled at her joke as did Roger and Marsha. He continued, "I know this is going to be good. If it tastes even half as good as it looks, I know I'll be back again."

Marsha spoke, "We have lots of repeat customers. I don't know what we'd do without Cat in the kitchen. Cat, are we caught up in the kitchen?"

"We are now, but I'll need some help getting the lunch items ready," said Cat.

"Okay, I'll be with you in a few minutes," Marsha said. "Could I talk with you for a minute or so? It seems you know all about me, but I don't even know your name. You are...?"

"It's Roger, Roger Pyles." He extended his hand to her, and they shook.

"Well, Mr. Roger Pyles. Could you tell me about yourself between bites of your breakfast and sips of coffee?"

Roger took a sip of coffee and a bite of toast, not burnt. "Okay, if you don't mind me talking with a mouthful of food."

She laughed, "Seems like most conversations here are like that. We thought of calling this place the Chat and Chew, but Umpa's won out. My boys called their grandfather Umpa, and so we named it after him."

"Catchy name. We had a Chat and Chew up in the area I came from, that part of America where you could be in West Virginia, Maryland, and Pennsylvania in less than ten miles," Roger said. "I was a college professor, Ph.D. in anthropology, who wore out my welcome at my school. About the same time, my wife and two-year-old son died in an auto accident. That was a year ago. I moved down here to a place I inherited from my father over in Canaveral Flats and was content being a hermit until Bill Kenney lassoed me like a free-range longhorn and talked me into helping him with the murder victim they found over in the swamp at Windover."

"Yeah, I read something about it in the *Florida Today* paper," she said.

"That's what your mom said, too."

"Dear old blabbermouth mom," Marsha said. "Did she say she'd pray for you?"

"She did."

"That's my momma and she will too."

Roger went on, "I bet she will. I can't say too much about an ongoing investigation, but it sure looked like a gruesome murder. I'm still waiting on the report from the coroner, but I can't see it being anything else. Keep this under your hat. I found a pin, a small black pin with two identical white letters on it. I think it was SS, but it was stylized for effect, and I'm not 100% sure that's what it is. I'd rather not say any more on this now."

Marsha said, "Alright, can't be too careful and let details out. How's your food tasting?"

"Great. I'm going to be one of your regular customers from now on," Roger said.

Just then, the phone rang and rang again. Marsha said, "I better answer that." She got up and grabbed it on the fourth ring. "Hello," Roger heard her say, but after that, could not understand much more of the conversation. She wrote on a small pad as she nodded repeatedly. After hanging up, she stuck her head in the kitchen and yelled, "Hey Cat, we have a big order. Construction company up at the power plant wants two dozen hoagies to treat their workers for lunch. We have an hour to get them ready. I'll be right in. No way you can do this without help."

Marsha walked back to Roger's table. "Mr. Pyles, I would love to talk more, but I have a business that is calling me. Can I take a rain check on some additional time conversing with you?"

"Sure," he said. "It would be my pleasure. And please call me Roger, okay?"

"Will do," Marsha replied. "I'll be busy in the kitchen getting that order ready so if I don't see you when you need to check out, just yell, and I'll come running."

"Okay," Roger said. Marsha disappeared into the kitchen, leaving Roger to eat his meal alone. The meal hit the spot, but his coffee cup was nearly empty. Roger saw the pot behind the counter and got it. He filled his cup at his table and looked at the man who sat behind him. Roger said, "Sir, could I freshen up your coffee?"

The older man looked at Roger with a mixture of curiosity and gratitude. "Why yes, thank you," he said.

"You're welcome," Roger said, and he set the pot next to his meal. He may need more coffee, and there did not seem to be any reason to return the pot yet. He made quick work of the remaining food on his plate, filled his coffee once again, and quickly downed the new cup.

Roger did a quick mental inventory for the dig today. He hoped to hear something from the coroner on the woman's death also. He rose from the booth and headed for the cash register. As he stood there, the old man got up, walked to the kitchen door, opened it, and said, "Fraulein Marsha, you have two men wanting to give you money. It would be best if you come soon."

Roger heard Marsha voice answer back, "Okay, Mr. Brachen. I'll be right there."

The old man nodded, closed the door, walked to the cash register, and stood next to Roger. "So, you're the unnamed man the newspaper said was doing the investigation of the young girl's unfortunate death?"

"Yes, I am. Wish someone else had the grizzly task, but it fell into my lap," Roger said.

"Two words of advice to you, young man. All things happen for a reason. God sees all, knows all, and will make all things right either here or in the next world," he said. "I could not help but overhear your conversation with the fraulein. Be careful. You never know where your investigation will lead you."

Roger studied the old man for a moment looking for a hint of guile but found none, so he smiled at the old man. "Thank you for that bit of insight, Mr. Brachen."

At that moment, Marsha came through the kitchen door. "Okay, gentlemen. Sorry to keep you waiting." She looked at Roger. "You had the special. That'll be $3.70 with tax. Got to make the governor happy too, ya know."

Roger handed her a $5 bill. "Keep the change," he said. She gave him a bright smile. "What does he owe you?" Roger asked as he pointed to the old man.

"He had the same as you did," she replied.

Roger returned the smile, but his had a bit of a grin. "Sir, it's on me, and I won't take 'no' for an answer." He handed Marsha another $5 bill.

The old man was surprised and said, "You really don't have to, but I feel I cannot talk you out of this act of generosity. So I say to you, danke sehr, or thank you very much."

"You're welcome," Roger said.

"Boys," Marsha said. "Sorry I have to run, but the last thing I need is two dozen hungry construction workers mad at me when they find they have no lunch. I'll see you both again soon. Bye." She hurried to the kitchen in the back of the restaurant.

Roger opened the door for the old man and held it for him.

"You are a kind man," the old man said. "Kindness will open many doors brute force cannot, but be careful, young man. Be gentle as a lamb, but wise as a serpent. There are wolves in sheep's clothing, and they could be right under your nose."

"Thank you for sharing your wisdom with me," Roger said. "Have a great day."

"You too, young man, and thank you again for buying my breakfast."

Roger nodded, and the men went their separate ways. Roger walked to the truck and opened the door. K9 had eaten all the food, not even leaving a morsel on the floorboards and was asleep on the front passenger's seat. After climbing in, he sat for a moment thinking.

The old man Mr. Brachen had lived a long time and seen many things in his life, but it seemed he wanted to share more than his earned wisdom. His words possessed an element of warning. What was the old man trying to tell him and why, or was it only his imagination?

Chapter 15

I am deathly allergic to cats. I mean, I love all animals, but they're not my animal of choice. Rick Hoffman

Roger pulled his truck onto US 1. The pungent smell of rotting seagrass, blown up by the east wind, filled his nose. "Pee-ew, that stinks," said Roger. The little dog raised her head and sneezed. "See? I told you so."

The traffic light at the Fay Boulevard intersection was green, and Roger took it. He drove past a Methodist church, crossed a double set of Florida East Coast Railroad tracks, made a left on Carole Street, and pulled into the parking lot of the Port St. John branch of the Brevard County Library System. He found a shady spot under a live oak tree as the day was growing hot and he was concerned about leaving the dog in the truck even with the windows open. Roger looped the chain through the steering wheel. "There, that should keep you out of trouble." The dog, which had been sleeping, opened her eyes to a sliver, sighed, and shut them again. "Why don't you just hang out a 'Do Not Disturb' sign?"

K9 continued her sleep on the truck seat. "Okay, fine. I was going to tell you to guard the truck while I was in the library. Some watchdog you are. A thief could steal my truck and you too. You'd watch him do it. Remember, I have three days I can return you."

The dog seemed to understand that statement somehow, crawled like a soldier under fire, and laid her head down on Roger's leg. She looked up at him, and her sorrowful eyes appeared to ask, "Would you really do that to me?"

Roger stared into those pleading eyes and knew he'd been had and busted. "Dog," he said, "you seem to have a way of seeing right through me. After the things Bill said about you for what you did to his truck, I had to stick up for you, you big galoot." He stopped and looked at the dog suspiciously. "You didn't do that on purpose, did you? Don't answer that. I don't want to know. You watch my truck, got that?" K9 gave a little bark that sounded to Roger like she agreed or just liked it when he talked to her.

He said, "Good, now we have that understood." Roger shook his head. "I've got to get out more. Here I am talking to a dog and acting like she comprehends and is answering back. Aye, yay, yay."

Roger got out of his truck and headed for the double doors of the library. An elderly woman riding a motorized scooter was having some trouble exiting with the heavy doors. He pulled the door open for her. "Thank you," she said.

"You're welcome," he responded and entered the building. To his right were shelves of VCR tapes for borrowing along with numerous books with signs 'Stellar Sellers, 7-day checkout' above them. A woman of about forty was emptying the last books from a rolling cart and putting them on the shelves. She wore a tight red skirt and a white ruffled sleeved blouse with a deep V neckline that revealed an ample amount of cleavage. Roger's eyes surveyed the layout of the library. The woman turned toward Roger and asked, "This your first time? Can I help you look something up?" And she smiled at him.

He looked at her name tag pinned to the blouse, and it read, "Connie." He smiled back. "Yes, I am looking for something, some information. My friend, Bill Kenney, told me to ask for Connie if I needed something and that you would be helpful."

"Bill said that?" she said with a bigger smile. "Why, that sly old dog? How do you know him?"

"We grew up together," Roger said. "And you might say he's my boss. He roped me into helping out with an investigation going on."

She asked, "So you're the new boy in blue who's helping with the murder. What can I do for you?" She chuckled.

He pulled the pin, now in a small clear plastic bag, from his pocket. "I need to know what one of these is. Have you any idea where we can start?"

"Oh, yes, I certainly do," she said. "Follow me."

She led him to a secluded corner of the library, stopped, and bent over for something on the bottom shelf. Roger looked at her curvy rump covered by the tight skirt. "I need some manly assistance. Can you help me with this?" she chirped.

Roger walked around the bent-over woman and reached down to the large and old looking book she was pointing to. He immediately noticed that her blouse had dropped down from the force of gravity and her ample bosom was visible. She wore a low-cut flesh-toned bra that hid little. She looked him eye-to-eye and said, "I believe this is what you want."

Roger said flatly, "I came in here for some information, nothing more. I see you would like to do it the hard way. I need to know about this pin, so please help me with this today and nothing more."

She still smiled, but it was a tighter smile. "Okay, maybe another day. I can help you with what you need. I know what that pin is and I don't need a book to tell me. It's a German Nazi SS pin."

"How can you be so sure?" asked Roger.

"My dad was in WWII. He had one of those as a war souvenir," she said. "He took it off one of those goose-stepping higher up officers along with his Belgian-made Ruger handgun and his nametag. 'Schnell' was the German's name. I remember Dad showing them to me as I grew up and wanted to know about his time in the war."

"So it is what I thought it is."

"Yeah," she replied. "Should be a number on the back to identify who received it. The only problem was when my dad tried to authenticate this with the government boys; they informed him all the records were destroyed during Allied bombings of Berlin at the end of the war."

Roger said, "Now that's a real bummer. Looks like I may have reached a dead-end, but I still think this could be the key to the whole case. I was hoping for an easy resolution on this pin, but as things usually go, two steps forward, one step backward. Looks like I may have to do it the hard way."

Connie smiled, "I think I'd like that."

Roger grimaced and then forced a smile. "Thank you for your help. I think I'd better be going. I've got some digging to do. We'll see where that leads me. Bye"

"Anytime you need some more help, especially the hard issues that may come up," she said, "I'll be available and at your service."

"I'll remember what you said," Roger said. "Gotta go," and he turned and hurried away. He zigzagged through the shelves of books, past the chest-high shelves which held VCR tapes ready to be checked out, and into the area with chairs and tables where the magazines and newspapers were. The man known as Brachen, whom he had just met at the restaurant sat reading a newspaper. He looked up at Roger and Roger nodded to acknowledge him. Bracken did the same as Roger passed. He went through the vestibule area and exited the building. Roger muttered under his breath, "Someone needs to throw a bucket of cold water on that woman."

He shook his head, walked to the truck, and climbed in. K9 lifted her head and turned to him. "Well, girl, let's head to Windover and see what we can find. Maybe you can help me dig for bones."

K9 gave him a doggy smile and a little ruff sound from her throat. "I agree."

He thought of Connie again. "Let's get out of here K9 before that siren tries to lure me in again with her charms. I think it would be the end of me just like for those ancient Greek sailors. Let's see what we can find in the muck. I have a good feeling about this, and my feelings are seldom wrong."

Chapter 16

The victor will never be asked if he told the truth. Adolf Hitler

The old man sat at the open-air bar at Stiltsville. His great joy had been broken with some disturbing news. The Finlandia Sahti beer he was enjoying now seemed to have fallen flat. How the deliverers had managed to keep this perishable beer cold all the way from where it was brewed in Finland, he didn't know. The cloudy beer with the yeasty and banana flavor set his taste buds in overdrive ecstasy, and now the moment was ruined for the old man, but he must carry on — loyalty, honor, and duty.

The Bear had reported to him that the man working the case of the young murdered woman, had in his possession a distinctive pin, an SS pin. It sounded to him like Valentino had indeed been busy again. Heyrich Reinhardt would pass this along to those who needed to know, and they would supply an answer on what action, if any, would be forthcoming. ODESSA had little patience in matters like this. It was and had always been an organization that valued secrecy above all. If anyone asked, they did not even exist. It was ludicrous to suggest they were anything but a rumor spoken by madmen and fools, but Heyrich knew better.

He looked up the Indian River and saw the Vehicle Assembly Building standing over 700 feet tall at Kennedy Space Center. Here, the giant Apollo rockets that took men to the moon had been assembled, and now they used it to join the boosters on the Shuttle prior to launch. He laughed to himself. All these had been created mainly with German scientists and engineers from the old Third

Reich who had picked the lesser of two evils when they surrendered to the Allies.

He'd heard of stories of those who had been captured by the Soviets. Those that they had no use for had been executed. Others, the Russians had worked till they dropped and died. Still, others were treated more fairly as they had information and brains too valuable to abuse and take vengeance on. Just the same, he was glad most had made it to the Americans or escaped the Allies' dragnet. With these escapees, those working for the Americans and a few for the Brits, the Third Reich could be rebuilt covertly under their very noses, and they would not even notice. That is if personal desires and personal agendas did not expose their plans. And Valentino was walking the razor's edge. He seemed to forget the overall strategy and think that he was too important to answer for his deeds and to be held accountable.

ODESSA would not let anyone or anything compromise the plan. They would make a decision. The Stork would be called to take care of the problem. He'd do whatever they told him to do and eliminate the complication with steely efficiency and ruthlessness. A chill went through Heyrich Reinhardt. He had seen and heard of work by the Stork. Only a madman would do what he did, and only a madman or a careless man would put himself in the crosshairs of the Stork. He was glad he was not in Valentino's shoes. It could go one of three ways. ODESSA would wait and see, but that was not their usual standard operating procedure. Still, you never knew. They had done things before that he could not understand the why or how.

They could send the Stork to neutralize Valentino if his liabilities outweighed his usefulness. Or they could take out the threat to their asset, Valentino. Heyrich Reinhardt was glad he did not have to make the decision, but he knew a storm was coming. He could feel it. Someone was going to die. It was merely a question of who and when. This much he knew, if the cover was ever blown, he was not going down with the ship this time. Loyalty, honor, and duty was the rule, but the rule be damned if it meant dying for nothing. For some, it may be a good day to die, but he had plans that could get him to tomorrow. His will to live was stronger than the broken record repeating 'loyalty, honor, and duty.' If a scapegoat and fall-guy were needed, it would not be him.

Chapter 17

Mystery is at the heart of creativity. That, and surprise. Julia Cameron

Roger drove his truck to the T-bone intersection with US 1 and waited for a green light. The pungent odor in the easterly breeze of the dead river grass rotting on the bank reached his nose again. It was just as bad as before. He wondered how people got used to it, but he remembered how the smell from a local paper mill back up home in the Maryland hills was a fact of life for all in the upper Potomac Valley. Fumes from the sun-dried vegetation had to be less of a health issue than the chemical odors from the paper mill at the town of Luke. He looked at the Florida Power and Light electric generation plant just to the south. Yellowish fumes poured from the twin stacks. *That certainly can't be any good for man nor beast.*

The light changed, and he carefully eased his way onto US 1. Glass and plastic in the road and some tire skids told his observing eyes of a recent accident. It seemed the right lane going north was a constant green through lane. You had to safely merge into the left lane, and someone had tried to do this in the right lane with less than desired consequences. He would not make that same mistake.

A new sign was up at a local park on the river to honor a fallen deputy hit by a car recently while chasing a fugitive at this spot. Being a lawman was a dangerous job. You never knew when the most innocent scenario could turn deadly. Across the street, he saw a large sign on a one-story building which read, "Grand Opening, Kelsey's Restaurant. 2 for 1 draft beer all day." From the full parking lot, it looked like things were going well for the new establishment.

He went past a second power plant owned by Orlando Utilities, a tall building with two stacks sticking out of the roof also belching out yellowish fumes. Another mile and he took a hard right turn on a cloverleaf of the NASA Causeway to head west. Going east would have put him at Kennedy Space Center in about ten miles.

He drove past another new sign erected by Brevard County for their newest park, The Enchanted Forest, full of old-growth oaks and longleaf pines and the unique sand ridge ecosystem. Two miles farther, he took a left into the new Windover subdivision and pulled into the limerock-covered parking lot. Roger got out of the truck, walked to the office, and went in. "Hello, Janet," he said. "How are things this morning for you?"

"Well," she said, "Mr. Man Who Keeps Banker's hours, I'm finer than frog hair split three ways."

"Now, that's very fine," he said. "What's got you in such a great mood?"

"Mr. Crane remembered my birthday," she said. "Got me a new leather jacket for riding on my Harley with my husband, and the old tightwad came through with the raise I wanted. My birthday has been great so far. Hope you're not going to rain on my parade."

Roger said, "No, just checking to see if the road to the crime scene site was open and passable. Guess he's not here from the way you addressed him."

"Mr. Crane's out in the field somewhere."

She asked, "Do you want me to find him for you? Do you need him for something?"

"No," Roger said. "It's all good."

"Speedy moved the backhoe out of the access road early this morning. He's somewhere on the south forty looking for a place to put the roads to the high hammock land that's suitable for building," she said. "He made sure the well points and dewatering pumps were up and running. And, oh, I think you will find this interesting. I got a call from the coroner. He said he called the University of Florida Archaeological Department. Seems the dean of the department, Dr. Marples, was vacationing in Cocoa Beach. He found out which hotel, made a call, got lucky, and reached him. Told him of the old bones. He was curious, came over to the coroner's office, saw the bones, and became very excited. The coroner said he told him they appeared at least four thousand years old, maybe up to eight or even ten thousand. He canceled the rest of his vacation and took the bones to Gainesville. The people there have been poring over them nonstop. They were too excited to sleep. They think we may have a find of historical proportions right here. How about that?"

"That's some good news. I'm sure surprised. Looks like I may have fallen into the find of a lifetime. They may need more than just my forensic experience on this one," Roger said.

"And get this," she said excitedly. "Old Dr. Marples, who rarely shows emotion, was so excited he called the governor and had him woke up in the middle of the night. The coroner said it got back to him, old Governor Grumpy Pants was none too happy at being roused from a sound sleep, but after hearing the news from Dr. Marples, he got excited too and said to keep him in the loop. If it was an ancient burial site, it was of major importance to the state and its history. He could talk to some people in the legislature about obtaining some funding quickly if the find was what they're hoping it was."

"Hmm," Roger said. "Looks like I need to get crackin' and see what I can find on the murder investigation and this new aspect. Seems we may all be on the state and even national news soon."

Janet said, "You never know. I'm going to have my hair styled, so I look good if Peter Jennings and ABC News show up."

"You never know." Roger rolled his eyes slightly. Major publicity is usually not something helpful on a murder investigation, but it could sure come in handy in getting the public behind state-level funding. Whatever happened, he had a job to do today. "Anything else I should know?"

Janet looked up and to the right before she met his eyes. "No, I think that's about it. Oh, Mr. Crane said to keep the walkie-talkie for now if you need it."

"Thanks, I will. Never know when I may need to contact you from out there in the swamp," he said. "Thanks for the information, Janet, and a happy birthday to you. Have many more."

"Thank you," she replied. 'Be sure to keep us informed of anything new of importance."

"I will," he said. "Bye."

At that time, the phone rang. She answered it and began to take a note. She looked at Roger, winked and gave him a thumbs-up, and went back to work.

Roger exited the office. *That was sure a surprise. Wonder if there will be any more?*

K9 was sleeping on the truck seat. She opened her eyes slightly to acknowledge Roger, and then closed them again. Roger shook his head. "Some watchdog you are." The little dog ignored him as dogs do.

He pulled out of the parking lot, drove down what would be the main road into the development, and turned right. He followed the trail as it twisted through the swamp and highland hammock. Roger came around a slight turn, and the thick vegetation along the side blocked his view of what lay ahead. A whiff of smoke crossed his nose, but he could not see it. As he neared the murder site, he saw two men sitting near a small fire cooking something. One was the man known as the Shaman. The other man looked to be sixty-plus years of age. He had long white hair tied in a ponytail that went down his back. He wore a red, white and blue bandana, a dirty, stained T-shirt and camo pants. A long white beard reached to his waist. He looked like a cross between a disheveled Santa Claus and Rambo.

Roger stopped the truck, wondering what to make of this. He had not expected a welcoming committee, especially not one like this. The Shaman ignored his arrival. He held a forked stick with what appeared to be several pieces of white meat hanging down cooking over the fire.

The white-haired man rose to his feet, but the Shaman remained seated, not moving. The white-haired man yelled at Roger, "We've been expecting you. Please come and eat with us. We want to talk to you about this development."

Roger did not like the looks of this. The odds were two to one, and each man carried a sheaved knife at his side, though he saw no guns. For all Roger knew, the white-haired man could have one hidden under his massive beard. He did see a spear about six feet long with a menacing-looking tip. It looked like the tip could be made from obsidian, but that mineral usually occurred in areas with volcanic activity like the western United States, not sandy Florida.

At that time, the little dog awoke, looked at the two men, and leaped through the open truck window on the passenger's side with the newly purchased chain dragging behind. Roger grabbed at the chain, but it went between his fingers, and the dog was gone. She ran up to the men and sat down with her mouth open and tongue hanging out next to the Shaman. He turned slightly, looked at the dog, took his right hand, and began to pet the dog. "Hello, canine," he said.

Roger knew if he wanted the dog back, he would have to follow. "Please come," said the white-haired man. "We mean you no harm."

Roger pulled the truck forward but stopped at a respectable distance. He got out and warily approached the men. The white-haired man had a big smile on his face and stepped forward. "Hello. You have to be the man the Shaman told me about." He stuck his hand out.

Roger took it and shook it. "I guess I am. My dog seems to like him."

The white-haired man spoke, "My name's Delbert, but most people call me Del. And yeah, Billy does have a way with animals. He don't say much, but when he does, it's worth listening to."

"His name is Billy?" asked Roger.

"Yeah, Billy Sawgrass," Del replied.

"He's the one they call the Shaman, right?" asked Roger.

"One and the same," Del answered. "I met him shortly after he came to the St. John River marshes from the big Seminole reservation down south. He'll answer to either name if he feels like answering when he's not in his slightly out of phase existence."

"Why did he leave?" Roger asked.

"He told me once. There were too many people there to suit him," Del said. "Like I said, he ain't much for conversation, but that don't mean he's not listening. He's still good company."

Roger looked at the Shaman as he gazed off into the distance and stroked the dog's fur. He stepped forward and stared at the sitting man. "He seems kind of spaced out. I hope my saying that doesn't offend him, but he does look like he's in a trance."

Del stroked his hairy chin with his hand. "He's well aware of what you said and what's going on around him, probably more than you and I are aware of. He's definitely different. Best I can describe it is; he's a little out of sync with this world or reality as we see it. It's different to him. He's a man of few words, but he sometimes displays rare insight on some matters. Sometimes it sounds like gibberish to me, but I wonder if it's just me not understanding what he is seeing and describing. Kinda spooky at times, but I've grown used to his ways."

Roger pointed to the spear. "Nice spear he's got there. What kind of tip is that? Looks like obsidian. Is it?"

"It is a well-crafted spear, just like his ancestors used to bring down mammoths," said Del. "He's a great flintknapper."

"Flintknapper?" asked Roger.

"Yeah, that's a person who makes the spear points," Del said. "Someone in the tribe showed him how and now he's the best of the best in this dying craft. You see, there's a few places in Florida where you find agatized coral. They take the glassiest parts, temper them with fire, and then make the sharp bi-faced coral heads. They can be deadly."

"I'd preferred not to find out personally," Roger said. "I'm familiar with how the ancient cultures made spearheads, but this material is new to me."

"I seen him bring down a hog with that very spear," Del said. "He's real good with the atlatl too. Seen him drop a deer at one hundred feet. That was a pretty sight."

"An atlatl?" Roger said. "He uses an atlatl? I've only seen them in museums, never in use in the wild."

"Well, he's good with that super-duper spear thrower. Damn good," Del said.

Roger said, "Maybe he will demonstrate for me someday."

Roger continued, "He startled me when he was here yesterday, like to scared me out of a year's growth. He walked right past me like I wasn't even here, over to where the backhoe dug up the human remains and said, 'The Ancient Ones are angry at what has happened. You must make it right.'"

Del let out a little whistle through his gnarly teeth. "That sounds like something he would say."

"Any idea what he meant?" Roger asked.

"That's a good question," Del replied. "Rarely does he say anything that's not a riddle or have two or more meanings. Whatever it is, sounds like you've been given a job to do. Hey, are you hungry? We got some bush meat cooking. Smells like it's done."

"What is it?" asked Roger.

"Cottonmouth, you know, water moccasin. This one had an especially bad attitude even for a cottonmouth and tried to get in our boat," he said. "We let him know he wasn't welcome, and now he or maybe she, is our grub. Sure is some tasty white meat. Just be careful and watch for bones. Snake got more little ones than fish. Hell, if you get one stuck in your gullet."

Roger said, "I've eaten some strange things in my life. My father was an old farmer who also liked to hunt. I've had brains and tongue and offal from many creatures that roam this planet. Closest I had to cottonmouth was a big rattlesnake my dad killed when I was young. My mom wouldn't eat it, but I remember it as being pretty good, but like you said, lots of bones."

"About the same," Del said. "Sit. I'll get our plates. Then we'll have some."

Roger sat on the ground next to the Shaman, and Del went to a dugout Roger had not seen. Roger tensed up as thoughts of Del returning with a gun crossed his mind. He was done for it if that was the case. Del reached for something in the dugout, and Roger was relieved when he saw it was banana leaves he carried. Del gave one to Roger, and the Shaman put the meat-laden stick in front of Roger who took off a small piece. "Don't be bashful," Del said. "Take some more. We have plenty from that big bad boy. They get fat when they were as long as he was. Bet the dog would like some too, but be especially careful about bones with her."

"Okay," said Roger. "I'll get some more for the two of us."

After Roger took what he wanted, the Shaman and Del got what they wanted. There was some still on the stick the end of which the Shaman stuck in the soft earth. The cooked white meat was tasty, and Roger gave some to K9 who swallowed it without chewing. The men said nothing as they ate. Roger broke the silence, "Say that was good. I was surprised."

"I told you it would be," said Del.

104

"Canine like you," the Shaman said, looking at Roger. "She wish to repay you with her life." He looked at Del. "Come. We must go. I hear their cry. We must answer."

All three men stood up. "What cry?" Roger asked. "I didn't hear anything. Who's calling?"

Del shrugged his shoulders. "Don't know, but if he says we must go, we must. Something's got his attention, and we need to find out what or who it is. Trust me, whatever it is, it's important. Sorry to eat and run, but the Shaman says to go, and I trust his instincts. Been right too many times. Got to go. Bye."

The Shaman picked up his spear, and the two men went toward the dugout. The Shaman turned to Roger and spoke, "The Ancient Ones are restless. You must tell the story, Roger Pyles."

The hairs on Roger's arms stood at attention. He watched the two men get into the boat, paddle away, and disappear into the swamp. The little dog sat next to him, watching too. He looked at K9. "Strange men," he said to her. "I don't think we've seen the last of them. It's already been an interesting day. Wonder what's over in the muck waiting for discovery?"

Chapter 18

The voyage of discovery is not in seeking new landscapes but in having new eyes. Marcel Proust

The two men had barely gone when Roger heard a vehicle coming down the rutted road. As it came into view, he could tell it was boss-man Bill Kenney and that he had a passenger with him. The truck stopped behind Roger's truck, and the two men exited the vehicle and walked up to Roger. "This place is beginning to resemble Grand Central Station. Wonder who else will show up, the Pope?" Roger said.

Bill asked, "So, Mr. Crane and Speedy have already been around?"

"No," Roger said. "The Shaman and his friend, a fellow who said his name was Del, left not a minute ahead of you."

"Del, an older guy with long white hair and a long white beard?" asked Bill.

"Sounds like him," answered Roger. "Bad teeth too?"

"Yup, that's Del. I've encountered him before," Bill said. "He lives out there in the swamp somewhere. And he sometimes has been seen in the company of the Shaman. He's harmless and sometimes even helpful, a Korean War veteran. Got shot up over there and the government gave him a partial disability which he lives on, that and whatever he can find in the river marsh. State boys don't like him. He kills whenever he runs out of can goods, in or out of season, and fishes without a license, an expletive deleted license, if you hear him describe it."

Roger and the other man laughed at Bill's description.

"How many other characters are out in the swamp I should know about?" Roger asked.

Bill rubbed his jaw with his left hand. "There's others out there. Hard to say how many. They come and go. You have the regulars, some of which you rarely see, mostly because they don't want to be seen. Some are hermits, a few are Indians like the Shaman, and then there are the ones hiding out from the law. You usually don't see them, but they're there. And then you have the hardcore poachers, the air boaters some of which are sober though many aren't, the fishermen, the kayakers, and general Americans recreating on the river and the surrounding swamps. That enough info for you?"

Roger nodded, "Sound like the run of the mill motley bunch."

"They are," Bill said. "Hey, where are my manners? I forgot to introduce you to my cousin Tom Kenney from back home, up in West Virginia." He looked at Tom. "Tom, this is Roger who's heading up the murder investigation for me. Roger, this is Tom."

The two men shook hands. "Pleased to meet you, Roger," Tom said. "Bill has told me quite a bit about you and the case."

"And pleased to meet you too, Tom," Roger said. "So, he's your cousin, and you know him well. I have to tell you to take everything he says with a big grain of salt. You did know he won the Liars' Contest at the Barberville Pioneer Settlement Fall Festival and also Cracker Christmas at Fort Christmas the last three years in a row?"

Tom was surprised and laughed. "I did know he could tell some farfetched stretchers, but I didn't know he was so professionally good at it."

Bill broke in. "It comes honestly from having hillbilly blood in me and from being a cop. I've heard so many lies and half-truths in my line of work. I can smell a lie before I hear it. I've heard them from the best over decades, and that's how I won the contests. I rolled all the good liars' characteristics and mannerisms together, and what do you know? I had a winner. Ding, ding, ding."

The men laughed.

"So, you haven't got the news from Mr. Crane?" Bill asked Roger.

"No," Roger said. "I did see Janet at the office earlier, but all she had was good news. What's up?"

"First, the bad news," said Bill. "Mr. Crane needs to pull the plug on this operation we have here for now. He needs the dewatering equipment for a project over on the other side of the development, but he has agreed to leave it here for today. So, anything we have to do or want to do has to happen today. This is now salvage archaeology and crime scene dig. There's no time for anything tedious. I don't know when we will be back if ever. Today's the day, Professor Pyles."

"Did you hear the governor has taken an interest in the dig?" Roger asked. "Maybe able to get funding for a real archaeological dig operation."

"I did hear, but don't hold your breath when it comes to money from the state," Bill said. "Too many special interests all screaming for the governor's attention. You can't count on wishes and promises from them. And you think I can lie."

The men laughed again. Tom said, "Yeah, and I'm supposed to be on vacation, and here I am being put to work, hard work in the Deep South heat, at that."

Bill said, "Tom, I know you want to go fishin,' so, tomorrow Roger is taking you out on the Indian River where there are *no* alligators. Trust me, no lying on that. I've been told you'd rather avoid them."

"That's right," Tom said. "Those creatures are the things nightmares are made of."

"Hey!" Roger growled. "What do you mean I'm takin' him fishin' tomorrow? My plans were drowning my sorrows with the liquid elixir of life, not drowning worms or baitfish."

Bill said, "There's also a shuttle launch tomorrow, and I need someone on the river to keep order. It's been delayed twice already, and you know what they say. Three's a charm. You'll have my Jon boat with the Canaveral Flats Police Department logo on the side."

But I don't have a fishing license or any police clothes," Roger whined.

"No one will bother you in the police boat, especially not the game warden," Bill said. "He owes me anyway after his boat motor conked out, and I towed him in. You can fish if you want and take a cooler full of that elixir of life too. I just ask that you put on of those insulated covers around your bottle or can. Make what you are doing, not too obvious. I'll loan you my police baseball hat, too, and you'll look real official while you drown your sorrows and your worms."

Roger said, "I hope that's all the bad news. Have any good news for me?"

"I do," Bill said. "The coroner called with his findings on the woman you dug up here. Your suspicions were right. She was strangled with the rope and from behind. And there was evidence of rape. He also found something else of interest; a pubic hair that would not have matched the body, which as you know, was shaved clean as a whistle."

"That is interesting," Roger said. "He may be able to get a blood type from the hair and even find some DNA."

"We'll be lucky if we can get the blood type," Bill said. "That new DNA testing seems pretty farfetched if you ask me, expensive too and time-consuming. Don't know if the county will go for it. We'll have to see."

"I hope they do go for it," Roger replied. "I think DNA is going to become much more important to forensic science in the future."

"Say," Tom said. "You have a fine looking dog there."

"I got her over at the pound," Roger answered. "They were going to put her down, but I got her on her last day."

"Seems strays of many different species looking for a home have a way of finding me," Tom said. "What's her name?"

"K9," Roger said.

"I know she's a canine," Tom replied. "What's her name?"

"It's K9 as in the British sci-fi series with the Doctor," answered Roger.

"Who?" Tom questioned.

"That's the one," Roger said.

Tom was puzzled and said, "Has anyone told you, you talk in riddles?"

It was at that time Roger realized the confusion he'd created. "If you don't mind," he said, "I'll try to explain later. We need to quit talking and start digging. Mr. Crane has a business to run, and he has already gone above and beyond what he had to. He could have bulldozed the site and said nothing. It's happened before."

"He's right," Bill said. "I think Mr. Crane is a man of his word and I would like much more to have him as a friend than as a foe. I think people up to and as high as our governor would like this to go smoothly with a minimum of waves. So, let's get the shovels and get to work. Roger, you did bring the camera?"

"Of course," he said a little miffed. "This isn't my first shindig."

"Good. Take lots of photos to document this best we can," Bill said.

"Okay."

The men grabbed the shovels out of Bill's pickup, worked out a plan of attack. Bill and

Tom would dig in the lower area where Speedy's backhoe has cut a deep gash, and Roger would work where the woman's body was found. He would look for any additional evidence involving the crime and anything else he may come across. The mucky peat was stringy, filthy, and heavy.

It was hard going, and the men's shirts were soon drenched with sweat. Tom stabbed his shovel into the black earth and hit something. He thrust again. A 'thunk' sound came as he hit the hidden resistance. "I found something!" he yelled.

Chapter 19

There are two possible outcomes: if the result confirms the hypothesis, then you've made a discovery. If the result is contrary to the hypothesis, then you've made a discovery. Enrico Fermi

"Well, keep digging. Use the garden trowel," Roger said. He snapped photos as the digging continued.

With care, Tom removed the black earth around the find. Many gray, heavily discolored bones slowly appeared as the muck was removed. Roger said, "Looks like you hit the mother lode. Sometimes, the ground will shift over time, and you'll find something like this. It happened that way once when I was on in a bog dig in Scotland or was it in Wales? It can be like a mixed-up puzzle." He continued to record the excavation with his camera.

Something that appeared to be a round rock protruded from the peat. "Looks like you found another skull, Tom. Let's treat it with respect. Could be one of our ancestors. You never know."

Tom said, "It was someone's ancestor. I will be gentle." He pulled the head bone from the muck and showed it to Roger. "What do you think?"

Roger looked at the skull closely. "My trained eye tells me, you've found the remains of a woman, probably a young woman. Find the coxal bone, and we will know for sure."

"The what?" Tom asked.

"The hip bones," Roger answered.

"Oh, yeah. That would make it easy," Tom said. Roger grinned. Tom got his drift. He dug, and more bones appeared. They were placed in the white plastic buckets one after the other, but no hip bones were among them.

"I think I found another skull," Tom said with excitement in his voice. Sure enough, it was a skull, a small one.

"Looks like you found a child's remains," Roger said as he snapped away.

Tom said, "Shame the young have to die, even the ancient ones."

"From what I've seen, it was all too common an occurrence up till modern times," Roger said.

Bill, who had been watching silently, broke in. "Hey, it seems to be getting wetter."

"Probably a spring that feeds this pond," Roger said. "Let's move over some and not go any deeper. Maybe farther away will solve our problem."

Tom and Bill moved away from the growing wet spot and returned to digging with the shovels into the dark peaty earth. They dug for a few minutes finding nothing until Tom's shovel connected with an object that made a 'ching' sound.

"Hey, I hit something. It sounded like metal," an excited Tom said.

Roger shrugged. "Could be anything. A piece of an abandoned kitchen appliance, old tin cans, auto parts, God only knows. Can't think those ancient people could work and make metal items. That's what usually makes a sound like that. Might even be something the killer left. Now, go slow and be careful not to damage any more whatever it is. Use the small garden trowels, and let's see what you found."

Roger snapped more photos as the other two men dug. Bill said, "There it is. That looks like an old gun barrel probably from a rifle."

The men dug in and, yes, it was a rusty gun. Roger put the camera in a waist pouch. He sprayed the gun off with the garden sprayer he had got yesterday from Bill. The weapon became visible. "I know what that is. It's a Shapes carbine," Bill said.

"How do you know that?" asked Tom.

"I've done some Civil War reenacting in the Sunshine State," answered Bill. "I try to make the annual event in February up in the panhandle at Olustee. The largest battle in the state took place there. Nearly 10,000 men fought a deadly and horrible battle, and the Southern boys prevailed." He stopped and began again. "That my friend is definitely a Sharps carbine. It was a favorite on both sides of the conflict. A lot of the soldiers took them home with them after the war."

"I'm more familiar with the events and guns of the French and Indian War when our home area was settled," said Tom. "Look, there's something else sticking out from where we pulled the rifle." Tom began to dig where he saw the object.

"Someday," Bill said, "I'm gonna have to explain the difference between a carbine and a rifle to you, but today's not the day. What've you found?"

"Don't know," Tom said. "Think it's a bone, a rib bone maybe."

"That does look like a rib bone," Roger said. He took several pictures. "Good guess. Let's see if there are any more."

As they dug, more bones appeared. Some were from an arm. One was the femur, the longest bone in the leg and it was very long. They also found bones from a hand and some vertebrae. All were placed in a separate plastic bucket. Bill looked at the assortment of bones and whistled through his teeth. "These sure look different from the other bones. They're not near as weathered or old looking."

As Tom dug with his hand trowel, he hit something hard which produced a dull thud. The two other men heard it and looked at the spot curiously. Roger snapped more pictures.

"Keep digging," said Bill.

Tom did just that very carefully. As he dug, a bony, round shape the size of a honeydew melon began to appear. "It looks like another skull, and it's missing a big piece."

He continued to dig and soon the object, a human skull, was pulled from the mucky black earth. Tom held it up and rotated it for the other two men to see. "Look," he said. "It's got a round hole on the other side."

Tom smiled as he displayed his find, but the other two men were not smiling. A look of concern covered their faces. Tom saw this, and his continence changed. "What? What is it? What's wrong?"

Bill looked at Roger, who said nothing. "That, my friend, is the kind of damage you find from a bullet. Whoever this was, and looking from the length of the femur, I'd say it was a tall man. He died from a gunshot wound. Gentlemen, I think we may have found another murder victim. And judging from what little I know about the aging of bones in the Florida earth and the Civil War era carbine with it, I would guess the man died from 1860 to maybe 1890. Gentlemen, we have another mystery."

"And we have another problem," Tom said. "Is it my imagination, or is this hole filling with water?"

Bill said, "Hey, it is. Roger, Speedy showed you how to check the pump. See if anything's wrong. I've haven't heard it running lately."

"Come to think of it," Roger said, "neither have I. I'll take a look."

He walked gently through the slippery soil to the industrial-size pump and checked its vitals. "Everything seems in order. Don't see anything out of the ordinary. Got gas and oil."

"Is the switch in the 'on' position?" asked Bill.

Roger looked at him like he had two heads. "Of course it's on," he said with some contempt in his voice. "First thing I checked."

"I had to ask," Bill said. "Can't tell you how many people I've helped over the years who missed the obvious."

"Sorry I snapped at you, boss," Roger said. "Guess the heat's getting to me."

Bill nodded but said nothing. Secretly, he wondered if Roger possibly wasn't feeling the effects of missing alcohol this morning. The water continued to rise at a visible rate. "Call Janet and see if she can raise Speedy and get him over here quickly to look at the pump. If it ain't fixed soon, we're not going to be able to work. This place will be underwater again."

"Will do," Roger said.

He called and got Janet who relayed the information to Speedy. He said he would be there ASAP. Ten minutes later, Speedy appeared and went right to work on the pump. The men dug feverishly as the water continued to rise and found more bones before the water forced them out.

The muddy men walked to Speedy. "Well, doc," Bill asked. "What's your diagnosis on the patient? Glad you make house calls."

"I can't find anything wrong with her," Speedy said. "She just doesn't seem to want to run. Probably something wrong with the electrical system. I'm gonna have to take the pump to the shop and tear into it. Do some diagnostics with a multi-meter. Sorry, boys, but I think by the earliest possible time I could have this back, the spot you are in will be under four or more feet of water. I think your digging has come to an early end."

Speedy looked at the diggers. All seemed to have a look of disappointment on their faces. Speedy said, "Sorry to spoil your fun, but I believe it's over."

The diggers said nothing for a moment. Finally, Bill spoke, "He's right. It's over for now. Let's gather up our tools and what we've found and call it a day here. Roger, you're free for the rest of the day, but I need you for riverboat duty tomorrow. I'll be over early with the boat and Tom, our guest fisherman."

Roger grunted, "Shanghaied again," and then smiled as he thought. Maybe he'd do lunch at Umpa's. Possibly Marsha would be there, and he could find out more about her.

Bill looked at Tom. "I'll have to find out what the coroner wants to do with these new bones we found. Mr. Crane will let me make a call at his office. After that, how about a pulled pork sandwich platter at Fat Boys BBQ restaurant? Sound good to you, Tom?"

"Sounds good to me, but let's get carryout," he said.

"We look like pigs, and the cooks may want to slaughter us, and then, we'd be on the menu, not ordering from it."

"Point taken," Bill replied. "I think you're right. Carryout for lunch and a much-needed clean-up to follow."

"Speedy, thanks for your help," Bill said.

"You're welcome," Speedy said. "Glad you're not too upset about the pump conking out."

Bill smiled, "Everything happens for a reason. Boys, this rodeo is over for us today, but our work on this is not. Tomorrow's another day. Let's make like sheep sh…, er, sheep droppings, and hit the road."

"Damn," said Speedy. "The rumors on you tryin' to stop cussin' are true."

"They are, "Bill said, "and you could learn to follow my perfect example."

This brought laughter from all, even Bill. Speedy disconnected the dewatering line from the pump and hooked it to the pickup truck. Bill and Tom put their tools and buckets with bones in the back of Bill's vehicle, and Roger loaded up the equipment that he had brought along with the little dog, K9, who had been watching the whole time. Roger was the last to leave. As he drove off, he looked in the rearview mirror and thought he saw movement in the bushes near the dig, but Roger had no desire to find out what it was, so he drove on without looking back again. He felt he'd had enough fun today. And tomorrow promised to be fun-filled also. Roger looked at K9. "Dog, what have I got myself into?"

Chapter 20

Let sleeping dogs lie. Robert Walpole

Officer Bill and Tom drove down the washboard street, Canaveral Flats Boulevard, known locally as CFB. Officer Bill's twelve-foot john boat with a small outboard motor stuck out past the truck bed, and it had the official-looking and highly visible Canaveral Flats Police Department decal on its sides. Up ahead at the turnoff to Roger's trailer, Bill could see an old black man with gray curly hair working on the fence. He wore some patched denim bib overalls and had a ragged straw hat on his head. Bill slowed his truck and stopped it next to the man. "Hello, Lester," he said. "How's life treatin' you these days?"

The old man smiled a broad smile. He had a mouth full of bright white teeth with one capped with gold. "Well, hello, Mr. Bill," he said. "If it gets any better, I don't know if I can stand it. And you, sir?"

"It'll be a busy day in this cracker version of Mayberry," he said. "How's my new man, my Barney Fife doin'?" He looked to Roger's trailer.

"Not too good, I'd say," Lester said. "Seemed awful hungover, if you ask me, and you did. I had to wake him up to let him know I was here to do the work he asked me to do. Told me in a slurred voice to go do it and not slam the bleeping door on the way out. He also asked me to feed his dog before he passed out in dat dilapidated La-Z- Boy chair. Good looking bitch, she is. She'd already tore a hole in the dog food bag and helped herself. Hope he don't blame dat on me."

"Thanks for the warnin', Lester," Bill said. "I'll get him movin'."

"You do that, sir," Lester said.

"How many times have I got to tell you not to call me 'sir'?" Bill said.

"You know why, sir," he said. "You know why."

"Yeah, I do, but I'd feel more comfortable if it was just 'Bill' or even something like 'Chief Bill,'" Bill said.

"Whatever you say, sir," Lester said through his smile.

Bill shook his head. "I'd better go. You can't get no work done with us jawin'. See you, Lester."

"See ya too, sir."

Bill shook his head again and started down the lane to Roger's trailer. "Sounds like you two know each other very well. What was all that 'sir' stuff about?" Tom asked.

"Me and him go way back," Bill said. "He was one of the first persons to buy property in the Canaveral Flats, and the local Klan didn't like it. They showed up one night in their sheets and hoods. Were gonna burn a cross in his yard and maybe burn down the little shotgun house he had built, with him and his family in it. My old man had his faults, but he treated everyone equally, good or bad. He believed just like the founder and developer of this little town that everyone should be welcome here, and Dad was willing to fight for that, if necessary. It wasn't too far from here just north in this very county, Harry Moore and his wife, Harriette, became the first Civil Rights martyrs when their house was blown up on Christmas Day in 1951. He wanted to make sure nothin' like that was gonna happen in Canaveral Flats. Lester had his revolver, and my dad had his double barrel twelve gauge Remington shotgun standing them off."

"Where were you when all this was going on?" Tom asked.

"Standing behind a big oak tree with my old man's twenty gauge aimed at the sheets," Bill answered. "I snuck out of our house when I heard the commotion. I knew Dad needed all the help he could get, and a skinny teenager can fire a gun just like a grown man, even if it woulda knocked me on my ass. Oops. I mean my butt. I think they saw me and some guns sticking out the windows of Lester's house. I learned later those were his kids' toy rifle pop guns, but the sheets didn't know that, either. The wolves got real scared and lost all their bravery when they thought the sheep were armed to the teeth. They made a bunch of threats. Said they would be back, but we never saw them again. I don't think they were locals, though they might have been."

"That's quite a story," Tom said.

"Yeah, my old man was mad. Said I could have got myself killed, but deep inside, I think he was proud of me and glad for the help, though he never would admit to the latter," Bill said. "Don't ever underestimate what a man can do because of his size or color."

"There's more, ain't there?" Tom added.

"Yeah, don't repeat this. Lester likes it to be a secret, but he's probably one of the wealthier men in the area. I think he has the first dollar he ever made. Worked his whole life as a member of the Laborer's Union. Never spent any money on himself 'cept maybe a good pair of work boots. Put a son through Florida Tech, engineering degree, and a daughter through the University of Florida. She's an OB/GYN doctor. After his wife died, all he did is work his day job and his side jobs, and watch an old black and white TV while sitting on the porch of his non-air conditioned house in a second-hand chair with broken springs in the seat. He's quietly helped a lot of people of all colors and all creeds, maybe even some who were there that very night."

Tom said, "He sounds like a good man."

"He is. Salt of the earth. He's one of the reasons I'm proud to live in and serve this little town that looks like Dogpatch. He was so thankful for my dad's help. He always called him 'sir' whenever he saw him. My old man told him not to do that to no avail. And he said to me as an honor to my dad he would continue calling me 'sir' like he did my dad."

They pulled up to Roger's trailer. Roger was sleeping soundly in the sorry looking chair. The little dog raised her head, looked at them, laid her head back down on her paws, and closed her eyes.

The two men exited the truck, walked to the screen porch, and went in. Roger snored. "Roger," Bill said. "Wake up."

Roger stirred, shifted his position on the chair, sighed, and began to snore again.

"Roger," Bill said more firmly. "We need you. Time to wake up."

He stirred again but was soon snoring once more. **"Roger,"** Bill yelled. **"On your feet!"**

Roger open one eye, looked around, and said, "You don't have to yell. I heard you the first time. I got to get a dog. Can't even sleep for all the interruptions from riff-raff. I got to get me a dog."

"You got a dog," Bill said. "Remember, she sh...., she took an unpleasant dump in my truck? Remember that dog?"

"Oh yeah, I did get a dog," he said. "Where is she?" He opened both eyes and looked at K9. "Some watchdog you are. You'd let them steal everything in the house, probably even show them where the good stuff is, and help them carry it away."

Bill said, "She helped herself to the dog food, too."

Roger got out of the chair unsteadily. "Woo," he said. "I think I need a drink."

"I got just the thing for you," said Bill. He handed a covered paper cup to Roger. "Drink up. It's just what you need."

Roger grabbed the cup eagerly and took a big gulp. His eyes grew large, and a look mixed with surprise and horror came to his face. He violently spat the white liquid from his mouth. **"Milk? Are you trying to poison me?"**

"I told you it was what you need," Bill said. "It'll settle your stomach. I also have a large black coffee, and hash browns and an Egg McMuffin from our local McDonalds. Eat up."

"Okay, I'll take it," Roger growled. "This is more compensation than what I expected from you, **Chief** Kenney."

Bill smiled, "Here's a twenty for some bait and whatever you need. Stop over at Stiltsville and get some shrimp and a six-pack, but no more. My boats gassed up and the fishin' poles are in the boat. Let's move it from my truck to yours, Roger. And I want Tom to drive. You're in no shape. Can't even stand upright and I don't want my new deputy getting picked up on a DWI. I would be the laughing stock of the county, and I've had enough embarrassment lately because of you."

"What!" Roger cried. "I'm not likin' this one bit. I don't want no DWI, but I'm doin' this under protest."

"Protest noted. Now, let's move the boat," Bill said.

With three men helping, the boat transfer went smoothly. Roger handed his truck keys to Tom. They hopped into Roger's truck with Tom at the wheel. Roger glared at Bill and said, "I told you, I ain't likin' this one little bit." He stuffed the breakfast sandwich into his mouth as they drove off.

"That went well," Bill said under his breath as he watched them leave. "Good luck, cousin. You're gonna need it. What could go wrong with this arrangement?"

He shook his head and looked at the dog on the porch. "And no comments from the cheap seats."

K9 growled and barked at Bill. "Okay," he said. "I'll give you another chance if you promise to be good."

She barked a more welcoming bark and wagged her tail. "Good," Bill said. "Now I hope Tom can get the growling out of Roger and he doesn't bite my cousin's head off. I think, dog, you're less irritable than your master." She barked again. "I second that, but Tom had better beware. His bite can be worse than his growl."

Chapter 21

I could resist anything except temptation. Oscar Wilde

Tom drove Roger's truck east on the washboard road laughing known as Canaveral Flats Boulevard. The road turned to potholed asphalt at Miller's General Store where the county maintenance began. Tom tried to weave his way among them, but couldn't miss all of them. One shook the truck severely, and Roger yelled, "Hey, you trying to kill me, or just wreck my truck?"

"Sorry," Tom said," Doin' the best I can. The road has more potholes than good pavement." He let that sink in. "Why would I want to wreck the truck? Not sure if you value your life from the way you've been drinking, but I value mine." Tom gave Roger a hairy eyeball.

Roger looked a Tom coldly. He turned his head and spat out the window. "Glad we didn't bring the dog with the way you are driving. You'd a jarred her liver out. Killed her, you would."

Tom saw an opening. "So, you like that new dog of yours?"

"Yeah, I do," Roger said. "She don't like Bill. She threw up and had a bad case of diarrhea in his truck. I cleaned it up, but it was everywhere."

"Yeah, he told me about the incident," Tom replied. "He was all animated when he was telling me the story, and I got a play by play description of what happened. I tried not to laugh."

Roger laughed and gave his Sam Elliott satisfied grin. "I would've like to seen that."

"He had three of those stinky air fresheners hanging from his rearview mirror," Tom said, "but it still didn't cover up the smell."

Roger laughed again and slapped his knee. "Serves him right."

The men drove on, and the road got better. Roger asked, "Do you know where you're going?"

"Not really," Tom said. "Bill gave such vague directions if I follow them; we'll more than likely end up in Cuba."

"We sure don't want that," Roger said.

"Wish someone would shoot that little tinhorn dictator Castro," Tom said.

"Be a waste of a good bullet," Roger said.

A harrumph came from Tom. "Probably right, but a lot of the people in Miami would agree with me."

"I think you're right. Enough about politics. You make sure you take a left at US 1, or we will end up in the Indian River, and this truck and all in it will sink like a rock. Comprender amigo?"

"Gotcha, we have to take a right at the main road, or it's hasta la vista," said Tom.

"That was a left turn. You know, hillbilly, the other right?"

"Oh, sorry," said Tom. "Make a left, the other right? Right?"

Roger nodded. "Glad we understand each other. Drive about a mile until you see the sign for the Port St. John boat dock. Turn there, and we'll take to the water like a duck."

"Sounds like a plan," Tom said.

The sign soon came into view, and Tom turned. The large lot held some trucks with boat trailers parked, but also many cars with people wandering around.

"Oh, yeah," said Roger. "Bill did say something about a Shuttle launch and for me to try to look official. Guess he forgot about the cop cap he promised."

"Guess so, but the boat has the official markings," Tom said.

"Well, that'll have to do today," Roger said.

Tom backed the truck up to the boat ramp and put it in Park. They pulled the boat out and slid it into the brackish water of the Indian River. Roger held onto the boat rope, and Tom got back into the truck and found one of the few remaining places open to park. He walked back to the boat, and the two men gently entered the boat as it rocked. "Wish I had a boat like that," said someone on the dock."

"Sorry," groaned Roger in his best Sam Elliott voice. "Official business."

Tom pulled the rope on the small outboard motor, and it started. He backed it out into deeper water, put the boat in neutral, and said to Roger, "Official business? That's some voice of authority you have, hombre."

Roger grinned, "Yup, got me in and out of a whole lot of trouble. Remember, that low life cousin of yours officially made me a member of the Canaveral Flats Police Department. What do you say we head for Stiltsville like he suggested and purchase the supplies we need?"

"All right," said Tom. "We're off," and he put the boat in forward and headed for the group of structures built on the barely submerged sand flats about a half-mile away.

The water was close to glassy. "Great day for a Shuttle launch, don't you think?" asked Tom.

"Couldn't be better, but I doubt the fish are biting much," said Roger. "Early morning is usually better."

"Just like up home," Tom said, "but it is what it is. Let's make the best of it while we try to look official."

"Yup," drawled Roger. "Got to try to look official for Chief Bill." He laughed.

Tom smiled at the reference to Bill. "And you're sure there're no alligators in the Indian River? I don't like them."

"Nothing to worry about. I've been told they don't like saltwater. Crocodiles do, but you'll only find them in extreme south Florida around the Keys," Roger said in his most reassuring voice. "Trust me on that."

The boat with a small outboard engine, an old Evinrude with a peeling fifteen horsepower sticker on the side, propelled them across the shallow estuary. Tom figured it must be a four-stroke from the noise it was making, but it could have been normal noise for a poorly maintained motor. Knowing his cousin Bill, he suspected both.

It was a short trip to Stiltsville. As they pulled up to the dock by the Tiki bar, three men sat the bar drinking a beer and watched the boaters every move. The one, who sat furthest away, was tall and thin and had a curious, malevolent expression on his face. They tied the boat up and walked toward the bar. One of the seated men said something to the others, got up, and greeted them. "Well, hello again, Mr. Pyles. What brings you to Stiltsville?"

"I need something. I was told I could find it here," Roger said. "Your name's Mr. Bracken, is it not?"

"Yes, I am the one known a Bracken," he said flatly. Roger noted a bit of what he thought was an edge in the man's voice, but why it was there, he didn't know. "What is this something you would like?"

Roger looked at him, somewhat surprised. "Why, beer and bait."

"Why, of course," Bracken said. "I should have known. What kind would you like?"

"How about a six-pack of Yuengling Lager and some frozen shrimp?" replied Roger. "What did you think I wanted?"

Bracken replied, "I was not sure. I saw the Canaveral Flats Police emblem on the boat and wondered. We don't often have a visit from the police. Chief Kenney usually lets us know when he is coming on official business."

"Does he?" questioned Roger. He let that sink in for effect. "In a way, we're out here today on official business. Chief of Police Kenney said I was to make a presence on the river today for the Shuttle launch."

"Is your friend an officer also?" asked Bracken.

"No, he's a cousin of Chief Kenney from up north down here vacationing, ain't that right, Tom?" Roger said.

"That about sums it up," Tom said. "Wife told me I needed a vacation alone to do some thinking and make some decisions. She's staying there to keep the home fires burning, so to speak. Kids and caring for my father, who has Parkinson's. Say, do you have any bottled water?"

"Yes," said Bracken. "Many come here to do just that, and yes, we do have some bottled water." His face had a thoughtful look. "Now, let me get the supplies you need so you can be off and about your business activities."

Bracken pulled a six-pack of beer, four twelve ounce bottles of water from the cooler and a bag of frozen shrimp from the freezer. He handed them to Roger, who asked, "So, what do I owe you?"

"Consider it on the house," said Bracken. "A goodwill donation to our local law enforcement and the goodwill Chief Kenney has built up with this establishment."

"Now, that is a surprise," said Roger. "Didn't know ole Bill had any goodwill built up with anyone." The men laughed at the remark.

"You might be surprised," Bracken said. Almost as an afterthought, he added, "How is the investigation going with the dead woman?"

"I can't say too much on an ongoing investigation, but I can say I am making good progress," Roger said. "I'll just keep pluggin' away, and with a little luck, I believe the pieces will fall into place."

"That is interesting news," Bracken said. "I won't keep you any longer from your duties. Maybe you can use a little of your luck with the fish today."

"How right you are on that," Roger said.

The two men put their supplies into the boat and were off. They went about one mile north on the water which how had a slight chop to it and had turned murky from the wind's churning. They stopped and anchored east of the Orlando Utilities Commission power plant. Lines were baited, and each man had a beer in his hand. Most of the boats gave them a wide berth as they passed.

"Guess we waited for a fish to get hungry while we try to look official," Tom said.

"Yup, that's about it. Looks like OUC has gone environmental. No more visible smoke from the plant," Roger said. "I read they were changing over to natural gas from that Bunker C crude oil from Venezuela. That stuff's about as nasty as you can get, but it's cheap."

"Think the other plant just south of here will change over?"

Roger laughed, "The FPL plant? Those people running the company are about as cheap as Scrooge if not cheaper. That place will burn the cheap junk until someone makes them change and I don't see that happening anytime soon with the bunch we have running things in Tallahassee. Best government money can buy."

"Now where did you learn that?"

"In the newspaper, where else?"

"The newspaper," Tom said. "You must be kidding. I saw a month's worth lying unopened on your porch."

"Yeah, it was in the newspaper. I do let them pile up and then feel guilty about not being informed." He laughed. "I go on a binge, and speed-read them all and throw them away." He stopped, and a sarcastic smile came to his face. "You know, you can believe everything in the paper."

"Right," Tom said with scorn. "It's all true. All of it."

"Why, Mr. Kenney, I think we have something in common. Only a fool believes it's all true."

Tom looked at Roger sideways. "It sounds to me like you have some experience with that."

"Yeah, some time ago in Miami a bunch of bad cops who should have been fired instead of being passed from one agency to another in Dade County, caught up with a dude on a motorcycle who had been on the run for hours one night down there. Dude had on a full helmet, full leathers, and gloves. It was like a feeding frenzy. The cops, all white, got carried away and beat him to death with their Billy clubs. When they got the helmet off of him, they found out he was black. The paper down there turned this cops gone bad story into a racial thing. Miami burned for days, and numerous people died before peace was restored. So yeah, I take stories in the papers and on TV with a big grain of salt."

Tom said, "Me too. Seems like they like to spin stories to sell papers and then claim no responsibility for the trouble their fairy tales cause." He finished off the bottle of water he had been drinking.

The men sat quietly for a while as they waited for a bite that did not come. "Hey, what's that?" asked Tom as he pointed to something floating and moving on the water's surface.

"What's what?" asked Roger as he finished his second beer.

"Over there. See it. It's coming closer. What is it?"

"Don't know," Roger said. "Well, I'll be. I think it's an alligator."

"Thought you said there were no alligators in saltwater. Where did you find that out, the newspaper?"

"As a matter of fact, yeah," Roger said. "You sure can trust everything in the paper as gospel."

"He's coming closer. What do we do?" pleaded Tom. "I ain't likin' this one bit."

"Can't say I am either. He's studying us. Don't show any fear."

"That's easy for you to say, Roger."

Roger said, "He's not too big, just a five or six-footer. I think he'll keep his distance and if he doesn't, I'll whack him with the oar."

The gator swam closer, but kept his distance as he passed and swam away. "I'm feeling much better," Tom said. "I was afraid I was going to be the third man in history to walk on water."

Roger chucked at the remark. "I'm glad he stayed away. I wasn't looking forward to a close encounter of the giant lizard creature type today."

Tom nodded. "Anything else in this river that can kill me you haven't told me about?"

Roger shrugged, "Well, there are sharks."

"Sharks," exclaimed Tom. "There're sharks in these waters?"

"Yup," replied Roger. "On one of my few sober days in the last year, I went for a ride around the county. Ended up at the boat dock we launched from. From the way an older man was talking to three teenage boys in a sixteen-foot Jon boat, I could tell he was their father. He gave them a sawed-off baseball bat and told them to make sure they killed any sharks they caught before they drug it into the boat this time. I thought he was kidding so after the boys left, I asked him about it. He told me the last time they boated up to their home in Titusville; the boys caught a six-foot shark and drug the thrashing and chomping beast into the boat with them. Not a pretty picture, but somehow they managed not to get bit. That's how I found out there were sharks in the river, not the newspaper this time."

"So is there anything more I should worry about out here?"

"We could drown in this water hazard."

"Very funny. You should get a job as a comedian."

Roger grinned, but for once in his life was able to bite his tongue and not say anything caustic.

The two men sat quietly thinking about the event that has just happened. A boat sped by a thousand feet away. "So tell me Tom Kenney, cousin of the illustrious Chief of Police in this fair town, what brings you to this point in time in central Florida?" asked Roger as he finished off another beer. "R and R is one thing, but I believe you've more on your mind than having a good time."

"There is. Got lots to think about. Lots of decisions to make. How much do you want to hear?"

Roger smiled, "All of it or as much as you would like to share. I've been told I have a good listening ear, and believe it or not; I can keep my mouth shut at times."

"Alright, Doctor Freud, wise in many things, but not alligator habitat, I came down here to clear my mind and get a perspective on things I have to do. The factory I was working at recently closed down, jobs are scarce around the old home area, and I need income. It's not like I'm gonna starve. I saved up a bunch of money to carry us for a while. I could see the writing on the wall with the plant closing. I've been thinking about goin' into business, the bottled water business to be exact. I see it's catching on here."

"Yeah," said Roger. "Bottled water does seem to be growing. I saw it in the market the other day. It might work out. Tell me more."

"I already have a building, and I can get the treatment and bottling equipment cheap from the old closed down Queen City Brewery in Cumberland, Maryland. There's a big spring on my property that's been supplying refreshing mountain spring water since the early settlers and Indian roamed the area and probably before."

"Sounds like you've put a lot of thought into this," Roger said. "It could work. What about customers? You need someplace for people to buy this."

"I know," Tom said. "I'm working on that, but I think I can work out the details."

Roger nodded. "Sounds like a workable plan to me. I think you could make it go. I'd give it some more thought, write out a plan, and then do what it takes to make it happen."

Tom smiled, "Yeah, I think it could work, too. I can see it. Even got a name picked out, Knobley Mountain Spring Water. What do you think?"

"Does have a catchy name. If the water is as refreshing as the name, you could have a winner, Tom Kenney."

"Thank you, Roger. I needed an unbiased and neutral opinion."

"You're welcome."

"Well, what about you, Roger Pyles? What's your reason for being here?"

"I ran away from my troubles. I expect Bill told you about them," Roger said.

"He told me a little," Tom said, "but I'd rather hear it first-hand from you."

"I guess it's only fair," Roger said. "Like you, I grew up and lived in that part of the world where you could stand in West Virginia, and if you had a really, really good arm, you could throw a rock over Maryland and hit Pennsylvania. My dad bought this piece of land in Canaveral Flats and put the trailer on it. We used it as a base camp when we came and vacationed in Florida. I inherited it when he died. That's how I got the property. How much do you want to know?"

"Whatever you want to tell. Fish ain't bitin', the shuttle's still on the ground unlaunched, and there's two beers left, one of which I'm gonna drink before you drink them all."

Roger sighed, "You know how to hurt a guy, but I guess I should share."

Tom rolled his eyes as he grabbed a beer. "You were saying....."

"Oh, yeah. I was one of those crazy kids who whenever they saw roadkill or an accident, did not look away when my parents said to. They just fascinated me as weird as that may seem to you, so when I went to college, I got degrees in forensics and archaeological stuff. Went all the way to a Ph.D. in it and was happily teaching at Western Maryland University. I helped the police up there solve several crimes. Not bragging, but I was good at what I did."

Roger stopped and took a big swig of beer. "Met a young woman who was the best thing and the worst thing to happen to me. She became my wife, and we had a son. That was the best part. She got me thinking, questioning things. You know, seeking truths. You would think those would be good things on a college campus, but it got me in trouble with the higher-ups when I began to ask my students to do the same. Varying opinions weren't welcome, and

130

they tried to get rid of me. People who thought different were a threat to them. That, in some people's eyes, was a terrible thing, but I'm so glad she had me thinking again and not just puking out what I was taught, and then I fed it to my students to swallow."

Tom said, "Yeah, seems like you can do your job well, but if you don't look and smell the same as the rest of the sheep, you will see the unwelcome mat."

"That's what happened to me. They tried to throw me out and keep me from having tenure. Fortunately, I had some aces up my sleeve that prevented this. Not everyone who finds themselves in this situation does. They offered to give it to me if I would just go away quietly. I was too much of a pot-stirrer for that, but when my wife and son died in an auto accident, it took all the fight out of me, and I took their offer. Since then, I've been living in Canaveral Flats trying to drink the pain away." He stopped and took a big swig of beer. "And now, grudgingly, I'm helping Chief of Police Bill Kenney try to find who killed the young woman out at the Windover site where you helped us and found the mangled skull and the gun."

"That's quite a story," Tom said. "I don't know how I'd react if I lost my wife and a son. It must be a living hell."

"It is. That's why I drink to try to kill the pain. Sometimes it works for a while, but it never goes away for long."

"I don't mean to make light of your troubles," Tom said, "but I believe everything happens for a reason."

"Sounds like something my wife would have said." Roger smiled slightly. "She was a good woman. I ain't much of a believer, but she was, and I trust she is resting in the arms of her Savior, but as for me, I not sure He exists and if He does, I'm mad at Him for taking the best things that ever happened to me from me. With the confusion and pain in my heart, now can you see why I drink?"

Tom sighed, "Yeah, I do. It's hard to understand why bad things happen to good people. Guess old Job could tell us a thing or two if he were here today."

"Yeah, think you're right, Mr. Tom Kenney. Guess I'm in stage 2 of gettin' over a loss. Maybe time will heal it, maybe not."

"I used to think that way, too. You see, I got shot in Vietnam, saw many men die horrible deaths. I can still hear their screaming in my head and see their blood and broken bodies. Why I survived, and others did not, I don't know."

"Everything happens for a reason; I once heard a wise man say."

Tom smiled, "Yeah, it's easier to advise than live it."

"Ain't that the truth?" Roger lamented.

The two men sat quietly in the rocking boat. The wind had picked up to give the water a moderate chop. A flash off to the east caught their eyes. Out on launch pad 39A at Kennedy Space Center, the Space Shuttle was rising with fire from her engines in the tail and from the solid rocket boosters hooked to her side. Thick white smoke billowed where the yellow-red flame ended and left a smoky, rolling plume as she rose into the blue Florida sky. It arched slightly to the east as the shuttle rose over the Atlantic and rolled as she struggled and fought to make orbit. The growling rumble from the sky beast became a roar. The men watched as did people they could hear cheering on the river bank. A minute passed as she rose higher, and then the solid rocket boosters separated to the sides and became their fall to the ocean slowed down by two large parachutes which deployed. The Shuttle attached to the external fuel tank continued on until it disappeared from sight.

"How's that for a show like none on earth?" Tom said with excitement dripping from his voice.

"Jim dandy," Roger said. "Won't see something like this up home."

Tom nodded. It indeed was a sight both men would remember for the rest of their lives. "Well, what do we do now? No way we can top that?"

"I think we need to stay out here, you know, look official like Bill said," Roger replied. "And besides, I need to finish this beer I just started." He grinned widely.

The men sat down and checked their lines, but neither had even a nibble. Roger sipped on the last beer while Tom drank from the bottled water container. He looked at it carefully, and Roger could hear the gears turning in Tom's head.

"How's the investigation into the young woman's death going?" asked Tom.

"I'm making some progress, but seem to have hit a dead end on my most important piece of evidence," said Roger.

"How so?"

"I found a pin in her hand, a pin I've identified as a WW II German Nazi SS pin, but what's it doing in Florida? It's got a number etched on the back to identify the owner, but those in the know tell me the records were all destroyed in the bombing of Berlin."

Tom looked at Roger, then towards the tall Vehicular Assembly Building at Kennedy Space Center, then back at Roger. "Ever heard of Operation Paper Clip?"

"No, can't say I have. Is that something like an office supply shop?"

"No. That benign-sounding set of words was what our government called the operation to ferry German space scientists, some of them very guilty of war crimes, over here to work for our faltering space program against the Russians, and also to sanitize their records. You know, the ends justify the means logic."

Roger said, "Tell me about it. I'm with you. What more you got on that?"

"Seems a lot of those German scientists ended up at Kennedy Space Center. See the connection?"

Roger nodded, "I do. You know anything about how I could find out who's SS metal that was?"

"Don't let the cover story of the records disappearing stop you," said Tom. "It's another of their ways for covering up the war crimes of some of the scientists. The records are there. You have to find out how to bypass the government's smokescreen. A friendly mole on the inside might be helpful, but don't look at me. I don't know any."

"How do you know this?" asked Roger.

"My dad was an Army clerk and shuffled papers for Operation Paper Clip," said Tom. "That and the fact I've met the father of the American Space Program, German-born Werner von Braun, twice. He used to fly gliders out of the Cumberland Regional Airport. Dad won a glider ride for two people, and von Braun was our pilot. He and Dad had a tense conversation on the plane. I was young and did not understand what they were talking about till years later when von Braun crashed a glider on the mountain behind our house near Short Gap. He said two things I remember, 'Bose Menschen ungestraft bleiben,' which means evil men go unpunished, and 'Not all the men from Germany who your government brought here are sheep. Some are still wolves dressed in sheep's skin. Beware.'"

"That would explain a lot. I know the saying. I took two years of German as an undergraduate." Roger said. "What if one of those men is still carrying on his own private, little war here and is still killing Jews? The only thing the woman had on her body was a necklace with a menorah and Star of David charm. It makes sense."

Tom turned his head sharply and said excitedly, "Hey, what's that?" He pointed to something large and grey in the water nearby.

"Where?" growled Roger. "I don't see nothin'."

"There! Can't you see it? Looks like a sea monster!"

This had Roger's attention. The grey blot got ominous as it came closer. A whiskered muzzle broke the water and blew out air vehemently. **"It's a monster!"** cried Tom.

Roger looked at Tom with disgust. "That ain't no sea monster. That's a manatee, you ninny."

"A what?"

"It's a manatee, a sea cow."

"You sure it won't eat or harm us?"

"No, it won't eat us. It's a vegetarian. Loves to eat seagrass and humans in boats with outboards are far more dangerous to him than he is to us. They're gentle giants, and this one seems interested in checking us out. Watch him and learn."

The manatee nosed around the boat using his broad tail to maneuver about. He used his two short arms like flippers to bring food to his mouth, which he eagerly devoured. He worked around to Tom's end of the boat where the anchor line was. The boat made a lurch forward.

"What was that?" asked Roger.

"Don't know," said Tom.

The boat lurched forward again harder. Tom looked at the 1000 pound beast next to them and exclaimed, "Oh, sugar. The anchor line's wrapped around his flipper!"

Before the curse could slip from Roger's mouth, the boat lunged forward violently. "Hang on!" yelled Roger and hang on they did as the beast pulled the boat around like it was a child's toy. After what seemed like an eternity, but was probably only tens of seconds, the rough ride ended. Somehow, the manatee had freed himself. The boat settled slowly on the Indian River.

After regaining his composure, Tom looked at Roger and asked, "I thought you said they were gentle and harmless."

"Well, the article in the newspaper said they were," replied Roger.

"And you can always believe **everything** in the newspapers," answered Tom.

"You know the answer to that, Tom. I think we've been out here long enough looking official, and we're out of beer to boot. You've given me some great information today. Thanks, I'll have to see where it leads. I was always good at following a trail wherever it led, no matter how difficult. Hey, let's head back to the dock and go home. Better yet, let's stop at a joint, get some food for us and a brew for me. What do you say?"

"Sounds like the best idea you've had all day. Say, has anyone ever told you, you're a dead ringer for Sam Elliott?"

"Yup, happens all the time. Now, start the boat and let's get out of here before the world's only killer manatee returns," and that's what they did.

***

Meanwhile nearby at Stiltsville.

Three men sat at a table in a far corner at the bar. They spoke in hushed, serious tones. The fate of two men lives was in the balance. At least one must die. There was no question of that. It was a question of when. They knew how it would happen. And maybe two would need to die.

Chapter 22

What in the world is a hangover cure? Brian Wilson

After opening the new gate Lester Johnson had installed, Chief of Police Bill Kenney expected the worst when he drove down the lane to Roger Pyles' old trailer.

He had been awakened at 2 a.m. by a phone call from the Brevard County Sheriff Department by Deputy Yates who informed him two very drunken men were creating a nuisance at Riverside Bar and Grill. It was closing time, and the men were refusing to leave. They said they weren't done drinking and weren't going till they finished and quote, "Damn ready too." Claimed they were cousins and friends of Canaveral Flats Chief of Police Bill Kenney and if the deputies knew what was good for them, they would leave them alone. After a short conversation with Deputy Yates whom Bill knew quite well, to confirm he would vouch for the two men and a brief reading of the riot act via the phone to both Tom and Roger, Bill was able to talk Deputy Yates into driving the two men home in Roger's truck. Bill would give the deputy a ride back to his vehicle, which he did.

Bill didn't like to call in favors, but this was one time he had to. He did not need those two in jail with numerous charges against them, but Yates owed him from a particularly memorable occasion. A certain long-haired redheaded and red-bearded mountain of a man from western Kentucky loved to drink, and when Red drank, he loved to fight. The bouncers could not stop him and neither could the outmatched deputies, no matter how many men they threw at him.

Bill remembered the night he got the call for help. People were lying on the ground outside of the bar and inside. Chairs and tables were overturned, and a huge man was walking around looking for someone else to fight. Red spied Bill and beckoned him to come

136

on. Bill remembered swallowing hard as he cautiously approached the big man. He also was wishing he had ignored the call for help, but it was too late now. The big man stood his ground waiting for Bill to attack, but Bill stopped just out of reach. He looked the man in the eye and said, "Okay, you want to do this the easy way or the hard way?"

From the grin on the big man's face, Bill could see it was going to be the hard way. He remembered grunting, turning a little to the side and looking away, but always keeping one eye on his adversary. This surprised and distracted the big man for a moment as Bill eased his blackjack out of his pocket. With a lunge, Bill sprang forward and smacked the weapon across the big man's forehead with all he had in him. Red's eyes rolled back in his head, his knees buckled, and as he fell forward, Bill had to get out of the way of the toppling redwood, or be trapped under him.

A blow like that would have killed an ordinary man, but this gorilla was no normal man. Still, Bill was relieved when he checked for a pulse and found one. He handcuffed the man's arms behind him, roused him and marched him out the front door on his tiptoes to the amazed Brevard County deputies. Since then, when the redheaded man got drunk and belligerent, the deputies would call for Bill to come. Whenever Red saw Bill walk through the bar door, he'd calmly turn around, put his hands behind his back, and wait for Bill to handcuff him.

Bill hadn't gotten any late-night calls involving Red in about six months, so he figured his construction job had ended, and Red had moved on, but the Brevard County deputies had not forgotten they owed Canaveral Flats Chief of Police Bill Kenney a considerable favor. Bill figured with letting the men off, the sheriff's department men would consider their debt to him paid in full and Bill had always liked to keep the tab in his favor, not even or owing anyone.

He was not in good humor as he drove toward Roger's trailer. Bill thought that his cousin Tom hardly ever drank more than one beer, but from what he saw, Tom was plastered last night. The deputy dropped off Mr. Rubber Legs Roger at his trailer before taking Tom to Bill's house. When Bill had returned from taking the deputy back to his patrol car, he found Tom sprawled out on his couch in only his underwear snoring loudly and drooling on his shoulder as only a drunk can. It was not a pretty sight, and he would hold it over Tom's head for some time. Tom was still passed out when Bill had left his home a short time earlier today.

He pulled up to the trailer and shut off the engine. Roger was kicked back in his La-Z- Boy chair sleeping like Rip Van Winkle. The little dog known as K9 was eating out of the dog food bag she had torn open yesterday. A five-gallon bucket containing water sat next to the bag and served as her water bowl. She wagged her tail.

"Well, dog, how's it going today? It looks like you have food and water. You still mad at me?"

He bent his hand down to pet the dog, but she growled at him, and he withdrew his hand quickly. "Okay, looks like you'll tolerate my presence, but you haven't forgotten and forgiven. I can live with that." He looked at Roger and said to the dog, "Your savior looks like crap. Grizzly bears have dumped better stuff over cliffs." The dog growled at Bill again.

"Okay, okay. You don't like it when I say this about him. Point taken. I can't put any of the blame for his condition on you. He did it all to himself with maybe a little help, maybe, from Tom."

She wagged her tail, barked at Roger, and then stuck her wet nose to Roger's and began to lick his face. He turned and said, "Go away," but he never opened his eyes. The dog continued to lick his face, and he tried to push her away, "Go away, I said."

He opened his eyes. "Oh," he moaned. "You ruined a good dream."

"Better get a dog to keep the riff-raff out," Bill sniped.

"Whatever," Roger groaned. "My head hurts, and my mouth feels like 10,000 camels were corralled in it."

"I don't know how your dog can stand your breath."

Roger looked at Bill through half-closed eyes. "Why don't you kick me again while I'm down?"

"Is that any way to talk to your boss and friend who kept you and Tom out of jail just a few hours ago? I had to pull in a lot of favors to make that happen."

"Oh, yeah," Roger said. "I kinda forgot about that. Thanks."

"You keep this up, and you'll be in the drunk tank for sure. And because of you two, all my hard-earned favors and goodwill with the local county deputies has now been spent."

"Sorry," Roger said. "I guess we kinda got carried away."

"If it weren't for me, you two would be behind bars and facing a bunch of charges."

"Like I said, I'm sorry. It won't happen again."

"It better not," Bill said. "I'm out of favors, and even if I had any more, I'd save them and not spend them on you guys again." His face had a look of disgust on it.

"What time is it?" Roger said.

"10 o'clock."

"Is that a.m. or p.m.?"

"The sun is out. What does that tell you, bubble-brain?"

"Oh, yeah. Sorry. It is light out."

Bill shook his head.

"Where's Tom?"

"Sleeping it off naked on my couch."

Roger's eyes widened. "And I thought I was a sight."

"You are a sight, and Tom's on my couch sleeping, but not naked. He does have on his tighty-whities."

"Even that's a mental image I don't want to see."

"Are you hungry, Roger?"

"Hungry? I could eat a bear."

"Good. I've got something in mind. Get your act together, and I'll take you out for a meal. Consider it some pay for your help and, besides, I need a progress report on the case from you."

"Maybe my day is improving."

"I thought you might be hungry now, so I have a chicken biscuit in my truck," Bill said.

"Okay, let's go," and he was up and out the door.

"Aren't you goin' to lock up?"

Roger looked at Bill like he was stupid. "Why? I got a dog to keep out the riff-raff now. Let's go. Where's that chicken biscuit?"

They got in the truck, and Roger saw the food in a clear plastic bag. He grabbed it and devoured it in seconds. "Got anything else?" Roger said.

"No food, but something else you'll need to improve the way you're feeling." Bill pointed to a tin pill container and a bottle of water. Roger opened it and saw some gray round pills and some white ones.

"What are they?" Roger said.

"The white ones are Tylenol, and the others are DGL, good for your stomach. Two of each should be enough. The gray ones are chewable."

Roger swallowed the two white pills and tossed the gray ones into his mouth. "Tastes like licorice. I like licorice."

Bill nodded. "That's what the 'L' in DGL stands for, licorice." When they got to the main road, Bill turned left.

"Hey, where we goin'?"

"I told you I was taking you to get something to eat. Now trust me, close the gate, and we'll get goin' to the restaurant, or we can sit here while I have to answer silly questions and your stomach cries out to be fed."

"If you put it that way, okay. Ain't never been out this way before."

"Then it's time you saw the backside of Canaveral Flats."

Roger quickly closed the gate and got back in the truck. "Let's go." And off they went.

The road was washboard in some places, but Bill did not slow down. They passed every kind of housing imaginable. Shacks with outhouses, RVs big and small, new and old, trailers, double wides and houses of all sizes, descriptions, and conditions were scattered along the roads through the swamps, palm trees, pines, and oaks. After the road doglegged to the right, they went by some inviting canals leading west, probably to the St. Johns River, and then took a hard left where the road sign indicated they were now on Satellite Drive. "This road looks like someone's maintaining it," Roger said.

"You're right. After a big school bus full of kids got stuck about a year ago, the school board went to war with the county about the road condition, and it's not been a problem since."

Roger said, "But isn't this road in the city of Canaveral Flats and not county road?"

"Shush," Bill said. "I know that, and you know that, but let's not ruin a good thing."

"Gotcha," Roger said with a smirk.

They rode on till they came to State Road 520, took a right, and one-half mile drive later pulled into the dirt parking lot of Lone Cabbage Fish Camp and Twister Airboat Rides. Roger looked at the haphazard building which seemed to have been thrown together with little forethought. "This is it?" Roger said. "Are we having fish bait for our meal?"

Bill rolled his eyes. "You're gonna get one of the best meals you ever ate. Oh, ye of little faith. Trust me. Have I ever led you wrong?" Before Roger could answer, Bill added, "Don't answer that."

Roger smiled and followed Bill into the building. This was definitely a one-of-a-kind type of place. The floor tilted at various, crazy angles. Bill sat down at a booth with a fake plastic Tiffany-inspired light with Budweiser printed on the sides. Roger took the seat across from him. An attractive waitress of about forty wearing a Lone Cabbage Fish Camp t-shirt and shorts placed two menus in front of the men. "Good to see you, Bill. It's been a while. I thought you'd forgotten me."

"How could I ever forget you, Sugar Plum?"

"What can I get you to drink?"

"A Coke for me and a beer for my friend."

"He's handsome, Bill. Do you want to order now?"

Before Roger could say anything, Bill replied. "Yes, get us a three-way sampler and one of those West Virginia platters, okay?"

She smiled widely, "Sure thing, a three-way and a mountain special. Coming right up." She grabbed the menus, turned, and walked away.

When she went into the kitchen, Roger looked at Bill. "A three-way sampler, what's that?"

"Gator, frog legs, and catfish. What did you think it was?"

Roger said, "Never mind." A moment later, he added, "She's an old girlfriend, this Sugar Plum?"

"Yeah."

"Sugar Plum? Why Sugar Plum?"

"You don't want to know."

141

Roger shook his head and said with some exasperation, "Sugar Plum. Are there any women in this county you haven't been with?"

Bill looked thoughtful and answered, "Oh, probably one or two."

Roger groaned. "Thanks for the beer, just the same. I wasn't expecting it."

"You're welcome."

"One more question; what's a West Virginia platter anyway and what's it doing in the Sunshine State?"

Bill said, "A West Virginia platter is a fantastic tasting hamburger covered in special sauce and coleslaw. And what's it doing in Florida? Owner's ex-wife was from the Mountain State. She started it as a special. It caught on and became a staple on the menu. It's still here even though she's been gone for years."

"Makes sense now," Roger said.

"Okay, then, tell me what you've found out new on the girl's murder case that I don't already know about."

Chapter 23

People need revelation, and then they need resolution. Damian Lewis

"Here's the summary," Roger said. "I haven't told anyone this, but I found some etching reagents and applied them on the SS pin and, as an afterthought, on the necklace the woman wore. Both had something engraved on them I was able to recover. The SS pin was a German WWII pin and had the number 175 on it."

"That's good news. You should be able to find out who received it."

"Your over-the-top friend Connie at the library helped me figure out it was a Nazi pin, but her information said the records had been lost during the war."

"Interesting," Bill said. "What did you mean by over-the-top?"

"Old gal came onto me like a cougar in heat. I was thinking of throwing a bucket of ice water on her to cool her down, or maybe a tranquilizer dart."

"That sounds like the Connie I know. I really should have warned you about her, but why ruin your fun?"

"Bill Kenney," Roger growled. "If you weren't my friend and part-time boss, I'd be very tempted to show you how much I didn't see the humor in what you done."

Bill could see Roger's neck tightening up and the veins on the sides starting to bulge.

"All right," he said calmly. "I won't do it again," but they both knew it was a lie. "What else?"

"I had an interesting conversation with Tom out on the river. I was telling him about the SS pin I found. It seems he had some privileged knowledge. Those records weren't lost after all. According to Tom, there was an operation after the war to bring German scientists, some of them war criminals, over here to work on our fledgling space program. The government sanitized their records and had been burying and stonewalling requests by various concerned groups about the men's actions during the war. The records are under lock and key somewhere with limited access to a select few."

"So, you think our killer could be working out at Kennedy Space Center right under our noses, hiding in plain sight?'

"Yep," Roger said, "and possibly our own government knows about him and is covering up for him in, as they might say, a national security interest."

Bill's eyes grew large. "That's some heavy-duty information."

"There's more," Roger said. "The necklace charm had a name and inscription on it I could barely read, but I'm sure I know what it said, most of it anyway."

"Okay, please go on. I knew my trust in you'd pay off." Bill looked at Roger and imagined Sherlock Holmes about to reveal a spicy tidbit. "What did it say?"

"'Mary Zimmerman, all my love to you.' There was a name as to who it was from, but I couldn't make it out. I know a couple of more tricks to try to find out who it was from, but it will take some time."

"Now, that's progress," Bill said.

"I have to thank Tom for his insight. He put forth the notion there's a Nazi wolf out on the Space Center for whom the war isn't over, whose killing off the unsuspecting sheep, possibly Jews, and has gotten away with it so far."

"My cousin Tom told you all that?"

"Some of it was from him. Some was mine, but the sum of both sets of information rolled together was greater than the components. I've seen it happen before in work I've done for the police and others."

At that time, Sugar Plum appeared with the drinks. "Sorry, it took so long. Some of the help called in sick today, and we're a little understaffed. It shouldn't be much longer for the meal. It will be worth the wait, I guarantee it."

The men nodded without saying anything, and Sugar Plum hurried off to take the order from another group of people.

Bill spoke first, "So, let me make sure I have this right. You think the murdered girl's name is Mary Zimmerman and we have a mad Nazi running loose carrying on his own little war on Jews and our own government or some organization in it is aware of his actions and is covering up for him. Is that correct?"

"It is. I know it sounds crazy, but this is where the evidence is leading."

"I agree. It does sound crazy, but I've heard of other cases that seemed less plausible and turned out to be dead on the money. This could be the big break we needed."

Sugar Plum rushed from the kitchen with both hands full of trays of food. She sat them in front of Bill and Roger, said the word, "Enjoy," and zipped off back to the kitchen.

Roger looked at the West Virginia platter in front of Bill and said, "Your burger looks and smells real good. Would you consider splitting it and I give you half the trifecta or whatever it was called."

"Sure," Bill said. "Glad you suggested it. That way we can share in the good stuff, and it's called a three-way here, not a trifecta, or threesome, or anything else. Check the menu if you want. Trust me."

Roger grunted. "I did and almost became a meal for cougar Connie, but I think I can trust you on this one."

Bill nodded. They split their meal. The food was delicious, but Roger noted Bill appeared to be lost in thought and ate little. "Hey, Bill," Roger said. "You gonna eat that before it gets cold?"

"Oh sorry, I do that sometimes. You got the gears spinning in my head, and I think I might know someone who can help you with a few answers. I have to make a phone call." Bill got up and walked to the payphone in the rear of the restaurant.

"Whatever," Roger grumbled with a mouth half full of food. He watched as Bill talked on the phone. He finished the last of his beer, caught Sugar Plum's eye, and pointed to the empty bottle. "Another, please," he mouthed. She gave him a thumbs up and dropped off a new bottle for him as she hurried by with a chicken platter in her other hand.

Roger was enjoying a frog leg as Bill sat back down. He said to Roger, "I was able to get ahold of an acquaintance who may be able to help you."

"I'm beginning to think you know everyone in this county."

Bill smiled, "I have friends in high and low places."

"I bet you do," Roger said. "Male and female."

Bill ignored his comment and asked, "How was the food?"

"Great, even better when it's still hot."

"I've eaten a lot of cold meals as a cop," Bill said and he chomped down on the burger. White sauce oozed from it and down the corners of Bill's mouth.

"So who's this person who may be able to help me?"

"Rabbi Katz."

Chapter 24

Not just Christians and Jews, but also Muslims, Buddhists, Hindus, and the followers of many other religions believe in values like peace, respect, tolerance, and dignity. These are values that bring people together and enable us to build responsible and solid communities. Alcee Hastings

Roger had time to think as he drove down US 1 toward Cocoa. The food at Lone Cabbage Fish Camp had been great. Bill had picked up the tab and, to Roger's surprise, had said nothing about the two beers. Bill took him home where Roger's truck with the police boat was still in it. Roger wanted to get the boat out, but Bill said to leave it. Another shuttle was scheduled to launch next week, and he needed someone "official" on the river again and yes, if Roger did not behave, Bill would not intervene for him again. He could talk his way out of any trouble he created. Bill went into his house and returned with the keys to Roger's truck. Bill said Tom was still snoring on the couch in his underwear. He gave Roger the keys along with a warning about drunk driving and instructions on finding the synagogue on Merritt Island.

Roger bypassed Florida State Route 528, known as the Beeline. He could have taken this route, but he hated paying tolls, and there was a $.25 charge to use the Bennett Memorial Bridge across the Indian River. Three miles later, he turned east on Florida State Route 520 and crossed the free, high-level bridge to Merritt Island. He took a right at the first light, Courtenay Boulevard, and drove two blocks to a white building that looked like a church except for the small sign that read "Temple Beth Shalom, House of Peace."

It had been a Baptist Church years before. The congregation had moved to a larger, newly built church that was required as population growth made it necessary. He parked next to a pickup truck and an older model Chevy in need of a paint job. It was breezy.

He found the front door unlocked and walked in but saw no one. A side door was open, and the light was on in what looked like the office. He heard talking behind another door and saw light coming underneath from a space where a threshold should have been. Roger walked in and surprised two men, one he took to be the rabbi, but the other man wore a skullcap more resembling a Kufi, a Muslim prayer cap. Both men jumped. "Oh sorry," Roger said. "I didn't mean to interrupt. I have an appointment with Rabbi Katz. Bill Kenney made it for me."

"That would be me," said the brown-olive skinned man. "Please wait in the sanctuary. I'll be done shortly."

"Okay," Roger said. "Very sorry to have intruded."

He shut the door behind him, walked to the main room, and took a seat. It was quiet, and he looked around in the sizeable unlighted room. It was pretty much like the old church it had been except a huge menorah, and Torah scrolls were on the raised platform, and various scenes from the Old Testament graced the stained glass windows of the building. One had Adam and Eve at creation. Another had shepherd boy David with a slingshot facing off the giant Goliath with his gigantic shield and sword, and another had Moses at the Red Sea crossing. A fourth showed Elijah taunting the prophets of Baal.

He realized this was the first time he had been in a house of worship since his wife's and son's deaths. He could see their closed caskets resting in the front of the church with a picture of each on top. Their bodies had been in no shape for an open viewing. Roger well knew how a body appeared from trauma sustained in an accident as they had. He sat solemnly reflecting and wondering what life would have been like if they had lived.

He heard a door open on squeaky hinges and then close with a bang. Roger stood up and walked towards the entrance to the office. It opened, and the Rabbi poked his head out. "Please come in, young man. I've been expecting you."

"Thanks, I hope you can be of help."

"That's why I'm here. Please take a seat.

Roger did and said, "I was surprised to see a Muslim here."

"He's a friend of mine."

"Your friend sure slammed the door on his way out."

"No, it's a windy day, and a gust took the door and slammed it. Sorry for the noise."

"Oh, I thought he left in a huff."

The rabbi smiled. "His name is Bashur, so he did leave with a bash." The men laughed at his little joke. The rabbi continued, "He's a Kurd who recently arrived in America escaping Iraq and its dictator Saddam Hussein. His family was one of the lucky ones who was visiting friends in a nearby town when Hussein's air force dropped chemical bombs on his village. He's been having a hard time adjusting to his new home both culturally and financially. We've been trying to help them."

"I would have thought he would be your enemy."

"He may be a Muslim, but he understands persecution and suffering as do the Jews," the rabbi said. "He's a good man, a proud man who I consider a friend. That being said, he's ashamed to have to take charity, and some of his own Muslims wouldn't like it if they knew he was taking aid from us. That's why he used the side door. Please, don't say anything about this. The secret belongs in this room."

"Got to admit I was surprised to see him here in the synagogue," Roger said.

"Mr. Pyles, I'm sure you know there are people of all religions who are good men. It's a shame whole groups are mistreated because of the actions of a few. My Torah tells me to show charity to the stranger among us."

Roger nodded.

"Do you know the story of Jonah?"

"The guy with the big fish?"

"He's the one. He was sent by Adonai, the Lord, to save his enemies. Jonah refused to go until Adonai gave him an attitude adjustment in the belly of the big fish. You can imagine the reception he had on the beach when the fish puked up the stomach acid bleached out Jonah. The people on Nineveh worshiped Dagon who was half-man and half-fish."

149

"Talk about a fish tale," Roger said. "I always thought God must have a sense of humor."

"He does. Esther is another example of this. Evil Haman died on the gallows he made to hang Jewish Mordecai."

"Yeah," Roger said. "My wife drug me to a Purim event at her church, but I have to admit, it was fun. We booed the bad guys and cheered the good guys."

"Yes, Purim is a light-hearted event about a difficult time in Jewish history."

"Believe it or not, Louis L'Amour used the plot in one of his short cowboy western stories I read."

"I did not know that, but it is a timeless story. Adonai wants us to show love and kindness to those who could be our enemies."

"Some of them could still kill you."

"It's a risk He wants us to take. He wants us to be as gentle as a lamb, but as wise as serpents." Just the same, I pray to Him for discernment on those who will harm us, and those who won't."

"Sounds like a good and honest prayer to me," Roger said.

"I'm glad you agree. Now, in Bill Kenney's phone call, he said he believed I could help you, Mr. Pyles. How may I be of service?"

"Bill Kenney, Chief of Police for Canaveral Flats, asked me to investigate a murder in his town. I found two important pieces of evidence. One is a pin with SS on it. I know it's a WWII Nazi pin, but I'm running into a stone wall from our government. The word is the records were destroyed during the war, but I believe it's not true. And I have a necklace with a charm you may be able to help me identify."

"I'd like to help you as a favor to the policeman. He's helped me in the past with some sticky situations. He's a man of many talents."

"So I'm finding out."

"Let me see the items," Rabbi Katz said.

Roger handed him them to the rabbi. His eyes grew wide upon seeing the SS pin, and he looked at it carefully as he rolled it over and over in his fingers. "There is a number on the back that should identify the owner."

"I know, and I think the owner and killer work at the Space Center. The government brought Nazi scientists with SS ties that I believe are unrepentant war criminals."

The rabbi looked up from the pin. "Mr. Pyles, I believe I can find out who received this item. I have some connections, call it a network of friends who have friends, but I must warn you to be careful. I don't believe you know the trouble this could cause."

"It's already cost a young woman her life, and she deserves justice. I want her to have it."

"Be careful, Mr. Pyles, and heed my warning. It may take a day or two, even longer, but I too believe in justice for all and I will help you. Now, what is so interesting about the necklace and charm?" He rolled it in his fingers. "Menorah on top, Star of David in the middle, and a fish on the bottom. You may think this is Jewish jewelry, but it's Christian. The fish gives it away."

"So the woman was Christian?"

"More than likely. This isn't something anyone would wear like the generic cross we see so commonly. It tells the story of how Christians believe they're grafted into the Jewish line." He rolled it over to the back. "Hmmm. Seems to say Mary Zimmer or maybe Zimmerman. Hard to tell. Zimmer and Zimmerman are German names and sometimes Jewish, but not always. Take Bob Zimmerman for example. He's Jewish."

"Who?" Roger said.

The rabbi smiled. "He's better known as Bob Dylan. You know, wrote 'Blowin' in the Wind' and 'Don't Think Twice, It's All Right' and many others.'"

"Yeah, I heard of him. Got several cassettes with some of his songs."

"That's the guy." He glanced at the charm. "There seems to be more writing on the charm, but I'm having a hard time making it out."

Roger spoke, "I believe it reads, 'All my love to you,' followed by the giver's name. I can't make the name out, but I have a trick I think will bring it out. I need time. It's not a quick process. Will take eight, maybe twelve hours. I'm planning on trying it tonight."

"I believe you are right on the inscription. Good luck with finding out the giver's name. It possibly could solve your murder. And you know we had some people named Zimmerman who went here some time ago. The husband's name was Eric, and I think, but don't quote me on this, her name was Mary or Miriam. I do remember they divorced, and Eric quit coming about that time, but I do believe I have his phone number. I could call him. It would be easier for me to ask questions of a sensitive nature, rather than you, a complete stranger."

"I would greatly appreciate it if you would and get back ASAP. I feel like something is about to break this wide open."

"Be careful, as I said, Mr. Pyles. There could be much danger on this trail."

"I'm thinkin' the same thing. Thanks. I'll be watchin' my steps."

"Good," Rabbi Katz said, and the smile left his face. "How can I help you? What's the true reason you're here today?"

Chapter 25

Auschwitz stands as a tragic reminder of the potential man has for violence and inhumanity. Billy Graham

Roger was taken aback. "What do you mean?"

Rabbi Katz smiled and said, "Your boss and friend is concerned about you and your well-being."

The two men said nothing for a moment. The rabbi broke the silence. "Bill Kenney sent you here for two reasons. One was to help you with the criminal investigation. The two of us go way back to when this county was heavily infiltrated with the Klan as was much of the South. He and another man with a name similar to his helped bust them, each in his own way. Besides Negroes, Jews were on their hit list. Many here are still alive today because of the behind-the-scenes efforts of Bill and the other man. I'd trust him with my life, and when he asks for a favor from me, he gets it. So, I will help you with your murder investigation and also your personal problems."

"That dog," Roger growled. "He had no business."

The rabbi raised his hand, commanding for silence and to Roger's surprise, he remained silent. The rabbi began, "I know why Bill sent you to me. You see, I know personal pain and suffering too. My wife of twenty years died suddenly. We went to bed one night, and when I woke in the morning, she was gone. She passed into the hands of Adonai quietly next to me, and I did not know till morning when I touched her, and she was cold. The doctors said her heart stopped, and that was that. I was devastated. I wanted it to be me who died and not her. I went on a bender of epic proportions and found myself on a dirt road in Canaveral Flats with a gun on my lap

153

and suicide on my mind when Bill Kenney found me. I still don't remember how I arrived there, but your boss risked his own life to talk me out of it. I could have shot him. I thought of how easy it would be to do something threatening and have him kill me, put me out of my misery. 'Suicide by cop' they call it, but he talked me out of it and saw I received treatment. So you see, I owe him my life. I can still remember what he said to me, 'Suicide does not end the pain. It just passes on to someone else.' That man is trying to help you more than you know."

Roger said nothing. He shifted uncomfortably in his seat and remained mute. The hardness in his eyes was gone, but the pain in his heart was real, and he had a lump in his throat. He said, "I feel like there's a darkroom in my heart where light will never shine again. Everything I valued and hoped for in life left the day my wife and son died. I drink to ease the pain. I drink because I want to die, too."

The rabbi nodded, "I know the feeling. I wish I could say after they dried me out, everything was different, and I never slipped back into depression and self-pity, but it was not that way for me. It took a long time for my recovery."

"My wife was a believer," Roger said. "Can you tell me why bad things happen to good people? Sometimes it seems like this god, who I wonder if he even exists, set all this in motion, but he's too big to worry about the details of what happens to us mortal creatures."

"Yes," the rabbi said, "I asked those same questions and more. I asked him why six million Jews died in the Holocaust. Why? For me, it boiled down to this. Did I believe Adonai is in charge of everything and all conditions or not? Did I believe He had a purpose in all this? Where is He in all of this? For me, the answers were something like this. Can a sparrow fall from the sky and He does not notice? He has a purpose in all this. He does, but sometimes only He knows why He does what He does and allows what He allows. Everything happens for a reason, but it took much time to get over the disbelief of this happening to me, and all the pain and the guilt of me surviving and her not. I found I must let go of the life I had planned and accept the one that was waiting."

A tear rolled down Roger's cheek. "I can tell you've been there, my friend. You've walked the walk on the path I've been on."

"Mr. Pyles, I don't have a twelve-step program for your recovery. For me, it was time and the prayers of others and finding my roots. This was my cure. I hope I have said something to help you find your way home."

"Thank you, rabbi." He sniffed his nose and wiped it on his sleeve. "I bet I must look a mess."

"You look and smell like a man who's drunk too much alcohol, been out in the sun, and not bathed for several days."

"Guess I must look and smell like a pig."

"You do. I've been there too, but keep the pig part to yourself. Jews and pigs don't go together well."

Roger smiled. "You've given me much comfort and things to consider. I've taken up too much of your time today. I think I'd better be going. Call me when you know something on the pin and necklace."

"I certainly will as soon as I have anything, but I would like to do one more thing for you before you leave."

"What's that?"

"Can I pray for you before you go?"

Roger thought for a brief moment. "Yeah, I believe I'd like that."

"Give me your hands" The two men grabbed hands and bowed their heads. Rabbi Katz spoke, "Y'-va-re-ch'-cha A-do-nai v'-yish-m'-re-cha; ya-er A-do-nai pa-nav a-le-cha vi-chu-ne-ka; yi-sa A-do-nai pa-nav a-le-cha.v'ya-sem-l'-cha.   Shalom."

"What does that mean?" Roger said.

Rabbi Katz said, "May Adonai bless you and keep you. May His eyes shine on you. May He be gracious unto you. May Adonai lift up his countenance upon you. And give you peace. Amen."

"Amen," Roger said. "Thank you, rabbi. I can see why Bill sent me here, both reasons. Can I consider you my friend?"

"Done," the rabbi said. "Remember, everyone has problems. Everything happens for a reason. And one more thing."

"What's that?"

"If your wife could see you now, what do you think she would say? Would she be happy with the way you are handling this?"

Roger grimaced and was silent for a moment. He met the Rabbi's eyes, "Thank you." He paused and said, "Thanks so much. I can find my way out."

"Goodbye, Roger Pyles. Go in peace. I will be praying for you."

Roger nodded. "Thank you, seems like there are people who still think I'm worth saving. Goodbye."

Roger let himself out of the synagogue and walked to his truck. He climbed in and sat down, but did not turn on the engine. The rabbi had given him much to think about and something else he had not seen coming. Hope.

Chapter 26

Get your facts first, and then you can distort them as you please.
Mark Twain

Morning, two days later

Roger reclined in his La-Z-Boy chair. It was 10 a.m., and it was already hot enough to fry an egg on a sidewalk in Central Florida including the town of Canaveral Flats, but it had no sidewalks or paved roads for that matter. Just the same, he was thankful for the screened Florida room and a fan. K9, the dog he got from the local dog pound, sat next to him sleeping. Roger sipped at a beer, his second this morning.

Through the trees that blocked his view of the main street, Canaveral Flats Boulevard, he saw a truck coming closer. It stopped in front of Roger's abode. A man got out, opened his gate, and started the drive down the lane to his trailer. He recognized the truck and the man who drove it. It was Bill. Roger had not heard from him recently and had been wondering when he would show up.

"Well K9, looks like long lost Bill's on the way. I'm sure news like this will make you happy." The little dog opened one eye, and a low guttural growl came from her throat. "I have the same feeling about him sometimes, and I know he's not on your favorite list. Just the same, try and behave yourself. I think underneath his rough and calloused exterior, there's a good heart beating inside his hairy chest." K9 quit growling, sighed, closed her eye, and appeared to go back to sleep.

Bill drove up and got out of his truck. "Well, look what the cat drug in," Roger said.

"And hello to you, too," Bill replied. He looked at Roger closely and noted he was sipping a beer, but did not appear drunk yet, as he had seen him regularly at this time of day on other occasions. "Been trying to reach you since yesterday, but you ain't answered your phone. Where you been?"

"Been here all day yesterday. The phone ain't rang once, and I have a witness. K9, how many times did that phone ring yesterday?" The dog continued to sleep. "See? No answer. The phone didn't ring at all."

Bill raised one eyebrow. "I don't think her answer would hold up in a court of law, but I believe you. Check and see if you have a dial tone."

Roger did as instructed. He came out of the trailer and said. "Line's dead."

"Probably been dead all of yesterday, too," Bill said. "I'll give the serviceman a call from the office. Did you check to see if it's plugged in?"

"Yeah, I did," Roger said. "Do you think I'm that dumb? And don't answer that question. When I didn't hear a dial tone, I did a quick check of the connections. All good. Got to be some problem outside of the trailer."

"Looks like we found the reason you haven't been getting your calls."

"Yeah," Roger said. "I'd been expecting some."

"You've had several, and fortunately the people calling knew I was the default option. They all called me after not being able to contact you."

"How many calls did I miss?"

"At least three, and they were all important."

"Okay," Roger said. "Don't keep me in suspense. Spill the beans."

Chief of Police Bill Kenney began. "The first call was from the coroner. The young woman was strangled, and there were signs of sexual trauma. She was raped. He found a pubic hair which obviously wasn't hers and we were able to get a blood type from it,

AB negative, not very common which should help us identify the killer."

"You sure know how to make understatements, Bill. AB negative is only found in six out of a thousand people. That's a big help. What else you got?"

"Rabbi Katz called after he couldn't reach you and he had big news. He found out who received the SS pin."

Roger said, "I ran my additional test on the necklace charm the victim was wearing. It did say Mary Zimmerman and the giver's initials were R. V."

Bill nodded. "It all seems to be coming together. The rabbi's contacts report SS pin number 175 belonged to a German officer named Randolph Valentine. Does that name mean anything to you?"

"Not really. Should it?"

"I've lived here on the Space Coast a long time and, yes, it does mean something. A man by that name is a real bigwig at Kennedy Space Center. He designed several of the structures and operations facilities there. I did some checking and found out he's a lady's man. Quite a Casanova."

"Randolph Valentine. Almost like Rudolph Valentino, the Latin lover."

"Exactly. Behind his back, he's commonly referred to as 'Valentino' by those who know him."

"Wow," Roger said.

Bill began again, "The rabbi also spoke to Eric Zimmerman, Mary Zimmerman's ex-husband. The rabbi said he was cautious in his answers but cooperative. Seems the sheriff's department had been around asking about her disappearance. Several other young Jewish women have disappeared over the last decade. He told the rabbi the divorce had not been amicable after she became a Christian, but he had moved on. Eric said he hadn't seen her in a year and he mentioned she had a rose tattoo on her ankle which could help identify her. Her middle name was Rose."

Roger's eyes widened. "I forgot to tell you or the rabbi about the rose tattoo. I forgot. I flat out forgot."

It was now Bill's turn to be surprised. "Double wow."

"What do we do now?" Roger asked. "This could get very sticky and sensitive."

"Very, but I took an oath to see justice done, and I take it seriously. I'm goin' to move forward with this information and let the chips fall where they may. I think we need to be careful. This could become very hairy. I'm taking this information to the state's attorney today. It'll be his responsibility once I give him our findings. He can also order medical records on the possible killer's blood type."

"I agree," Roger said. "I'll keep running this over in my mind and see if there's anything I missed or forgot."

"Do that. Make sure we dotted all the i's and crossed all the t's."

"Every jot and tittle."

"What?"

"The rabbi would understand. A jot and a tittle are the smallest letters in ancient Hebrew."

"Oh."

"I'll go over it all again, the smallest detail, with a fine-toothed comb," Roger said.

"Do that. We may need it if this thing blows up as I think it could."

"Will do. You said you had three calls. What was the third one?"

Bill smiled uneasily. "Glad my name isn't Roger Pyles."

"What are you talking about?" Roger asked.

"Sarah, Tom's wife called, and he answered the call while he was still very hungover from you two guy's escapades the other night. His dad's taken a turn for the worst, and he had to leave for home. I gave him a bottle of Tylenol and a thermos full of strong coffee before he left. She managed to get an explanation of why he was feeling so poorly out of Tom, and now she wants your scalp. Be glad there's a thousand miles between you and that Cherokee woman, and that I got the nasty-gram, not you."

"Got him in big trouble, did I?"

"I think you just made the understatement of the year," Bill said. "I met her at a Kenney Family reunion a few years ago. She seemed a good woman, very protective of all she found valuable. Tom told me it took a lot to get her mad, but to watch out when she went on the warpath. Fortunately, once she vented, she would be back to her old easygoing self, but you getting Tom drunk and almost arrested? If you know what's good for you, I'd keep my distance for now and approach her with cautious if and when you meet her."

"Thanks for the warning."

"I know what I need to do today," Bill said. "What are you up to?"

"Thought I'd read the last week of papers from the pile over there on the floor, go over the case again, and then do some reading on this book about Florida history I picked up at the library."

"Did that old lioness try to sink her claws in you again?"

"Fortunately, no. Connie wasn't working, and I was able to find what I want without being ambushed."

"My best advice on her is simply to tell her, 'No, I'm not interested in your wares,' and she'll typically look for easier prey. Usually, but you never know with Connie."

"I think I should thank you for that, but I'm not sure."

"I'm not so sure myself. Just the same, I've got to get goin'. I need to report this new information to the state's attorney and take care of the normal duties of Chief of Police in this fair town. You take care, and as I said, you be careful. If you come up with anything or need me, call me."

"Don't forget to call the phone company for service," Roger said.

"Will do," Bill replied. "I have a bad feeling this could be the calm before the storm."

"I do too, but I'm not sure we will see or feel the storm until it's upon us."

"Agreed. Something about this does not feel right."

Bill nodded. "See ya later, gator."

At that time K9 awoke and growled at Bill. "I think it's her way of saying goodbye to you," Roger said.

"I believe you're right. Places to go. People to annoy."

Bill climbed into his truck and was off. Roger watched as the truck disappeared down the washboard road. The dense and sticky humid Florida summer air had an ominous feel to it, and Roger doubted it was because an afternoon thunderstorm full of rain and lightning was coming. No, those were normal for this time of year.

Something else was happening. Something more like a Category 5 hurricane. He could feel it.

***

Later in the day at about 6 p.m.

Roger reclined in his La-Z-Boy chair, sleeping. An empty pint of Wild Turkey lay on the floor nearby. A loud honking roused Roger out of his stupor. He looked toward the noise coming from a truck on the street. A decal on the side read 'Southern Bell Telephone Company.' A hand from inside the truck beckoned Roger to come. He rose unsteadily from the chair and walked the distance to the truck. A man in work clothes exited the work truck and met Roger at the gate. "Are you Roger Pyles?" he asked.

"Yup," Roger answered. "And who might you be, Mr. Serviceman?"

"Ernie Wolff, phone tech for Southern Bell. I had a call in about a line out of service."

"Yup, that would be mine. You sure got here in a hurry."

Ernie said, "I was out here on another call in Canaveral Flats. The Chief of Police Kenney saw me and asked me if I could check into it now. Normally when people do that, I tell them to call the office and put in a request. Company policy and procedure, you know."

Roger smiled. "But let me guess. As a favor to good ole Chief of Police Bill Kenney, you did this for him."

"How did you know?"

"Seems half of Brevard County owes him favors. What'd he do for you?"

"It's embarrassing."

"I think I understand. Bill seems to have a knack for showing up at just the right time."

"Does he ever," Ernie said. "I was out in the back near the St. Johns River working on a line to a house at the end of what looked like a cow path by a canal. I'd been working up the pole for a long time and finished my task. When I looked down, I saw three gators with their mouths open at the base of the pole looking up at me with what I took to be a look of anticipation on their reptilian faces. They

162

say gators can't climb, but the one apparently never read the book which said they can't climb. He had half his body off the ground leaning on the pole, and he was looking right up at me. Needless to say, I stayed at the top of the pole.

I hooked into the phone line and called for help. Chief of Police Kenney showed up. He laughed at my predicament, pulled his gun out, and shot the biggest gator in the head. It thrashed around for a while before dying, and the other two took off like they were supercharged. I climbed down the pole, and he said, 'You owe me one. Want some gator meat?' The gator meat was good, but I don't know if he will ever consider the favor paid for. Anyway, I can't complain too much. I would still be up the pole if he hadn't shown up."

"Sounds like the Bill Kenney I know," Roger said.

"I checked on your feeder line from the local switching station box. The box was locked, but it looked like someone had disconnected a wire and attempted to make it look like it had come loose naturally, from expansion/contraction and road vibration. I want to check the lines at the trailer, too. I've worked these lines for a long time. Retirement is staring me in the face. I've seen a lot and whoever did this was a professional. Do you have any enemies, Mr. Pyles?"

"Looks like I do now," Roger said. "Why did you stay out here and not drive-in?"

"I value my hide, Mr. Pyles," Ernie said. "Half the people in this town have dogs with big teeth and the other half has huge dogs with huge teeth. Ever had to run from two charging Rottweilers?"

"No. Can't say I have or would want to."

"Once was more than enough for me," Ernie said. "I honk at the gate and wait for the owners to come before I do service. Safer that way."

"I can image. FYI, I have a small dog, and she's friendly to everyone but Bill Kenney, so you should be okay."

"Wonder why she doesn't like him?"

"Seemed to me it was a mutual dislike from the beginning. Dogs are like that sometimes."

"Cops too."

Roger grunted, "Yeah, some cops too. Now, let's quit talking and check the trailer lines out. Hey, want a beer?"

"So bad I can taste one," Ernie said. "But I get stopped with alcohol on my breath and in my company truck, I can kiss my fat pension goodbye."

"I don't want that. I'll drink mine and yours for you."

Ernie groaned, "Right neighborly of you. Let's get this done, and I can head for home and all the brews I want."

"Okay." Roger opened the gate, and the serviceman drove up to the trailer. K9 came out the doggy door Lester had recently installed wagging her tail. The serviceman patted her head and stroked her back. Roger showed him where the phone and the lines were. All checked out in order and functioning properly. Work completed, he drove up the lane and closed the gate behind him. As he drove off, Roger mouthed these words, "Someone out there does not like me. Think I'd better be watching my back. It's about to hit the fan."

Roger had no more than reclined in his old chair when he saw Chief of Police Bill Kenney's truck approaching. It stopped. Bill opened the gate and drove up to Roger's trailer. Bill got out, and Roger noted a sour look on his face. "Didn't think I'd see you again today. You look like your momma weaned you on a sour pickle. Why the long face?"

"I just came from the state's attorney's office. I had a long talk with him, and you're not goin' to like it. The bottom line is this; there ain't goin' be no charges brought against Randolph Valentine."

"What?" Roger cried. "We had more than enough for charges and a conviction."

"I know we did, and the state's attorney agreed."

"So what was the problem?"

Bill sighed, "Seems yesterday a bunch of G-Men from various alphabet agencies descended on the state's attorney's office and told him under no circumstances were any charges to be brought against Valentine and he was to keep anything that turned up like your findings buried."

"But why?" Roger said.

"What else? National security."

"Sounds more like a cover-up to me."

164

"You think?" Bill said with sarcasm. "Seems those government men have been one step ahead of us the whole time. I don't know how they got wind of all this, but they did, and they want it kept quiet or else. "

"I think I know what the 'or else' is," Roger said. "So that's it? We do all this work, find the killer and the all-knowing men, the feds, shut it all down and pretend nothing happened?"

"That about sums it up unless we can come up with something to force their hand."

"Any idea what it would be?"

"Not a clue," Bill said. "Those guys are holding all the aces, and we're like pawns to them in their game. If we did come up with something, it would have to be so big they couldn't deny it or cover it up, and even if we did have something huge, they could spin it, and Valentine would still get off scot-free smelling like a rose."

Roger groaned, "So that's it. We roll over and play dead."

Bill said, "I hate to say it, but for now, yeah. It's fourth down, and we need forty yards gain for a first down. So, we're gonna have to punt and see what kind of field position we get. Maybe they'll drop the ball, but I'd not count on it. The ball will be in their court, and we'll have to see what they do with it."

"Ain't fair," Roger said.

"I know it ain't fair. Stinks like a fresh pile of horse sh...., horse stuff," Bill said.

"That's all we can do?" Roger asked again.

"I afraid so," Bill said and he added, "With this development, there's all the more reason to be careful. We haven't seen the end of this by a long shot."

"I couldn't agree with you more."

Bill said, "I'm going home and get a shower. After my time with the state's attorney, I feel like I need one."

"Better use lye soap for the filth."

"I don't think he liked it any more than I did, but we're stuck with it for now," Bill said. "Roger, my friend, as I said before, be careful. Be very careful. I've been a cop for a long time, and I don't like what I'm seeing. There's danger ahead, big danger."

Roger could feel the hairs on his arm stand on end like it did when a lightning bolt struck close to him one time back when he was a teen and been caught outside in the woods during a summer thunderstorm. "I know you're right."

"I'll be goin'. You stay safe and let me know immediately of any changes, no matter how minor."

"I will," Roger said.

Bill said no more. He had to walk around K9, who was sleeping on the floor. He got in his truck and drove off.

Roger watched Bill go. Whatever was coming was near. For a hurricane, you can batten down the hatches, but this felt more like tremors before an earthquake. He was as ready as he could be and he'd have to ride it out until it was over.

Chapter 27

If you're going through hell, keep going. Winston Churchill

Ting!

Ting, ting, ting.

Roger opened one eye and could see rain falling in the light of a nearby streetlight. The gentle pitter-patter on the tin roof of the porch became a soft pounding as the rain increased into a downpour. He looked at his watch, midnight. The deluge continued for several minutes soaking everything not under cover. As quickly as it had come, the rain departed. Roger breathed in the rain-freshened air and was soon back asleep.

KABOOM!! Roger woke with a start. He looked at his watch at 3 a.m. Every dog in Canaveral Flats was now awake and barking, but K9 was violently pulling on his pant leg and making a desperate cry. It was a combination of pleading, crying, and whimpering. Unlike her, he knew what the loud sound was. It sounded like a transformer on one of the power poles had blown. It was very dark. Every light in the town seemed to be out. Roger shifted in his chair. At that moment, he saw the green light from a laser pass over him.

Reacting more by instinct than by thought, he rolled out of the chair onto the floor hitting hard. Bam, bam, bam. Three shots rang out as Roger tried to become one with the concrete floor. The dogs in the town barked even louder than before, and K9 crawled next to him and whimpered like a frightened child. "Quiet puppy," Roger whispered. "Shhhh." He put his arm over her back and drew her close.

The dogs of the town continued to bark. Twenty, maybe thirty seconds later, Roger heard a car starter engage. From the sound, he knew it was on a Chrysler product. A large engine typically found in a muscle car roared to life and thundered off to the east.

Roger and K9 lay still for a few more minutes before Roger felt the coast was clear and cautiously got up. He looked around and heard someone coming.

"Roger!" the voice yelled. "Are you okay?"

"Bill. Is that you?" Roger yelled back.

"Yeah, it's me. Are you okay? What happened?"

"I heard the transformer blow, and then someone tried to shoot me. I think he took off in a muscle car, probably made by Chrysler."

Bill turned on a high powered flashlight and shone it in the direction from where the loud noises had come, but he saw nothing unusual. He flashed it on Roger and K9 and then around the porch stopping at the shot up La-Z-Boy chair. "Looks like you're gonna need a new chair. Glad you weren't in it."

"Me, too," Roger said. "K9 was violently pulling on my pant leg for some reason, and when the laser light appeared, I immediately hit the deck and then the bullets came flying. If it hadn't been for her urging, I would have still been in the chair and full of holes now."

"Looks like your dog rescued you."

"The Shaman said she'd save me."

In the light from the flashlight, Roger could see K9 looking at him. Her tail was wagging, and she seemed to be giving him a toothy smile. Roger put his hand on her head and stroked her down the back. "Good dog," he said. "Good dog."

"Got any weapons here, Roger?"

"A .22 pump rifle for armadillos and squirrels and a .9 mm pistol. Why you ask?"

"Get the pistol 'cause we're goin' after the SOB that tried to kill you."

"I like that idea," Roger said with satisfaction in his voice. He went into the trailer and returned wearing a holster with his gun in it. He had a flashlight in his left hand. "Let's roll."

"Good idea on the flashlight," Bill replied. The two men walked cautiously toward where the transformer had blown. They saw nothing unusual until they got to the pole. At the bottom on the ground was a cut lock. Bill said, "Yup, that would do it."

"What would do what?" Roger asked.

"That lock was to keep any unauthorized person from disconnecting the power lines. You don't do it right, and you have fireworks. Some places you may be able to pull the plug this way, but not here with the FPL grid. This was either done by an amateur or someone not from around here and who thought all electrical systems were the same. Let's see if he made any more slip-ups."

The two men walked around, looking at the ground for a good minute. "Hey, I found something," Roger yelled.

Bill quickly came over. "What did you find?" he asked with enthusiasm.

"Looks like he stepped in a soft, muddy spot."

"Yup, he came this way, and...," Bill looked around, "and walked over to this tree, rested the rifle in this convenient tree fork, and let the lead fly. Look, I see a shell casing. He must have been in a helluva big hurry getting' out of here when his plan went south." Bill put a car key in the open end of the casing and dropped the shell in his pocket.

"I think you're right. He'd have a clear shot to my trailer from here."

Bill's radio at his side vibrated, "All units in the Port St. John, Williams Point area. Attention, vehicle on fire at Port St. John boat dock. Attention, all units in that area. Please respond. Witness reports a Dodge Charger engulfed in flames. Four Corners VFD is on the way."

Bill looked at Roger. "You did say you thought the car that roared out of here was a Chrysler product, didn't you?"

"Yup, I did. And Dodge is in the Chrysler family of cars. Are you thinkin' what I'm thinkin'?"

"I am. Our shooter's destroyin' evidence and we need to be on his tail, not here. This can wait," Bill said. "Let's take your truck to the boat dock. It still has my boat in the bed, and we may need it for a trip on the river."

"I agree. Let's go."

The two men ran as quickly as they could through the brush and darkness. They hopped in Roger's truck and made it to US 1 in record time though both men were nearly jarred out of their seats as Roger took the washboard road much too fast. He slowed for a red light at US 1, looked and saw no traffic, and ran the light fishtailing as he made the left turn. Immediately, blue lights erupted from the darkness at a gas station on the corner and gave chase. "What do we do now?" Roger yelled.

"Keep going," Bill yelled back. "It the sheriff's department and I'll explain the situation to them at the boat dock."

Roger nodded and floored the truck. The speedometer read 90 mph as they roared up the four-lane highway with the deputy's vehicle, siren screaming, and more flashing lights than on a Christmas tree erupting in hot pursuit.

Roger slowed at the entrance to the large parking lot for the boat dock, but the rear truck wheels still skidded as he made the turn. They could see a car with flames leaping high from it down by the far-right docks. Firemen from the volunteer fire department were spraying water on it from a respectable distance.

"Quick! Pull over there," Bill yelled as he pointed to the far left boat dock. "I got a plan."

Roger did as he was told. He decelerated quickly at the water's edge. He said, "This better be good."

"Trust me," Bill said.

Roger rolled his eyes as the Brevard County Sheriff's Department car squealed to a stop behind them. From somewhere in the darkness behind the glaring light, a voice demanded, "Hands out of the vehicle. Hands where we can see them, now!"

The two men did as instructed. Bill shouted, "Yates, is that you?"

"Who wants to know?" the angry voice challenged.

"Bill Kenney, Chief of Police for Canaveral Flats. That's who."

"Are you guys drunk?" Yates inquired.

Bill turned his head toward Roger. "Are you drunk?"

Roger could tell there was some doubt in Bill's voice. "No. I ain't had a drop since about 6 p.m. last evening."

"No. We ain't drunk. We're in hot pursuit of a fugitive that tried to kill my deputy, Roger Pyles."

"Why didn't you say so?" Yates said. "Fill me in on the details."

Bill Kenney quickly explained the events which brought them to the boat dock. While they were talking, one of the firemen walked up to Deputy Yates and asked him, "Charley, I think I know who done this."

"Go on," Yates said.

"When we pulled up here, a tall, skinny man was running to a boat. Another man was in it waiting. Even over the noise from the engine, I could hear them arguing and probably cussin' at each other in what sounded like a foreign language. They took off towards Stiltsville."

"Was it German?" Roger asked.

"Could have been," the fireman replied. "It sure wasn't Spanish."

Bill said, "I think we need to go to Stiltsville, Roger."

"Agreed," he said.

The two men hurriedly got the boat from the back of the truck to the Indian River and were quickly off toward the buildings on the sand flats a mile off. When they were halfway to Stiltsville, Bill cut the engine and said, "This is gonna be dangerous. Whoever shot at you is probably out there and would like to finish his job. Let's be ready for anything."

"Got that right," Roger said.

The words had barely escaped Roger's lips when angry yelling came from Stiltsville, followed by three quick gunshots. A tall man ran across the dock of the establishment and dove into the water. Another man appeared, staggered to the dock and filled the night air with the sound of automatic weapon fire as he shot at the first man swimming away in the darkness. The second man staggered back around the corner, and another blast from an automatic weapon split the night.

"Hold up," Roger said.

"You don't have to say that twice."

The men sat in the boat, waiting. A little over a half-minute later, an explosion erupted at Stiltsville and red, and yellow flames engulfed the building. Both men raised their hands in a protective gesture as a roll of heat, and thunder-like sound hit them. A look of fear passed between them, and they wonder what would happen next. There were no more explosions and flames consumed Stiltsville.

"Look, over there." Roger pointed to something bobbing on the water's surface. "Looks like a body."

"It does," Bill said. "Could be our shooter."

"Let's go slow," Roger said.

Bill nodded and pointed the slow-moving boat in the object's direction. It was a body. With the light from the fire, it was easy to see the object bobbed in the dead man's float, but they approached with caution. Roger could hear his mother's words in his head saying, "A dying cow can still give you a lethal kick." How right she was.

They watched the body for signs of movement. There were none.

"I think he's dead," Bill said.

"Me, too."

They pulled the boat closer, but the man did not move. With guns ready for action, Roger poked the man with his oar. He could see at least six bloody bullet holes in the waterlogged lower part of the jacket, but the face was intact.

"Looks very dead to me," Roger said. "Why's he floating? I thought dead people sank and stayed down till they bloated?"

"Don't know," Bill said. "Could be something he's wearing or maybe his lungs are still holding air." They pulled the body into the boat.

"Ever see that face before?" Bill asked.

"Yeah, I believe I have," Roger said. "I think this was the guy who was at the Stiltsville bar the day of the Shuttle launch when Tom and I purchased supplies. He was sitting with Bracken and another fellow I took to be the owner. They all seemed a little alarmed by our arrival. Guess I know why now."

"See anybody else around here?"

"No. Anybody still on Stiltsville is a crispy critter by now."

"Think you're right," Bill said. "Let's take our deceased passenger to shore. He has a date with the coroner."

"Wonder who he is?"

Bill said, "When we find his identity, we should have some answers to what's been goin' on, but I don't think the fat lady's ready to sing."

"Me neither," Roger said. "Me neither."

Chapter 28

The pessimist complains about the wind; the optimist expects it to change; the realist adjusts the sails. William Arthur Ward

Bang, bang, bang. "Open up."

Bang, bang, bang. "Open up. I need in now."

Fred appeared inside Miller's General Store. "We open at ten," he yelled.

"This is Deputy Roger Pyles. I need in this store now!"

Fred shuffled through the store as only Fred could and stared out the front door window of the General Store passed Roger.

"Fred," Roger shouted, "I need some supplies for a case I'm working on. Let me in."

"Okay, Mr. Pyles," Fred said. "We'll let you in. What do you need?"

"You have plaster of Paris in the store, Fred?"

'Yeah, we have some. What you need it for in such a big hurry? Couldn't you have waited till the opening time at ten like everyone else?"

"Fred, I need it for police work. I need to make a plaster mold of a footprint for someone I believe tried to kill me last night."

"Oh, in that case, we got all you need. So, you're the one who got shot at last night. We heard the shots right after the transformer exploded. Got any idea who did it, Mr. Pyles?"

"I think I fished his dead body out of the Indian River early this morning and no, I didn't kill him though. Someone got to him before I could even think of paybacks."

"Was he an ugly, tall, and skinny guy?" Fred asked.

"The fellow I hauled in could be described that way. Why do you ask?" Roger said.

"A man like that was here in the store two days ago. He was not nice. He called us stupid. We did not like him and were glad when he left. He asked where you lived too, but we did not tell him. We played stupid, just like he called us."

"Fred, did you see what car he was driving?"

"We did. It was one of those Dukes of Hazzard, General Lee cars."

"So, he was driving a Dodge Charger?"

"Yeah, a 1969, but this one was metallic blue, not red like the one on TV. We remember its license number. Do you need it?"

"Need it? Why, Fred, I could kiss you."

"Please, no," Fred said. "Momma is the only one we let kiss us, her and the dog."

"Fred, tell you what. Get me the plaster of Paris and a sixteen-ounce bottle of water and write down the license number. I think if you do that, I'll skip kissing you."

"Okay. A tip would be nice."

Roger handed him a $5 bill, and Fred's eyes lit up. "Thank you, Mr. Pyles. Here's the number from the car." He handed a slip of paper to Roger.

"Thanks, Fred. You've been more help than you can imagine. Gotta go. Got work to do."

As Roger turned, he heard, "Later gator." Roger turned to face Fred and said, "After a while, crocodile." Roger thought he saw a hint of a smile on Fred's face, but it was hard to tell.

"Tell Boss Hogg, Roscoe and Enos hello," Fred said.

"Will do, Fred, and thanks."

***

Roger found the place where the footprint of the suspected killer was in the mud, and it was still intact. He mixed the Plaster of Paris with the water he had purchased at the store after taking several refreshing mouthfuls of the liquid. Roger poured the mix into the shoe depression, making sure he filled all areas. Twenty minutes later, he pulled the hardened plaster up and was pleased with the first look. He wanted to compare it at the coroner's office with the boots the dead man had worn. A match was almost assured, but he had to know for sure. His stomach growled, and he realized in all the excitement, he had missed breakfast. A trip to Umpa's was in order.

***

Roger walked into Umpa's Restaurant. It was empty. Roger looked at his watch, 10:30 a.m. It seemed like the breakfast crowd had come and gone. The lunch crowd would not start for another half hour or so. He took a seat and Marsha came out of the backroom. "Why, Mr. Pyles. Good to see you again. Do you know what you want, or do you need a menu?"

"You can call me 'Roger.' Mr. Pyles seems so formal." He gave her a big Sam Elliott-type grin. "I'd like the biggest breakfast you got and coffee, lots of coffee. It's been a long night."

"Tell me about it. We were swamped this morning with all the excitement at the boat dock and with Stiltsville burning down. Don't think I ever saw so many cops and fire trucks."

"I was in on that. Want to hear it from someone who was there firsthand?"

"Yeah, I would, but let me get your order to Cat, okay?"

"Sure thing."

Marsha went into the kitchen. Roger could hear her talking with Cat, but couldn't make out much of the conversation. She returned shortly and sat down across from him. "Well, Mr. Pyles, I mean, Roger. What can you tell me about last night's events?"

"Roger sounds much better." The big grin returned to his face. "It all started at my place in Canaveral Flats at about 3 a.m. Someone tried to kill me. Took three shots at me and just missed. I heard a muscle car tear out and then we, me and Bill Kenney, heard that a similar car was on fire at the boat dock. We took off for there with the sheriff's department in hot pursuit, but that's another story. A fireman at the dock told us two men had just left the dock in the direction of Stiltsville. We got the boat in the water and took off toward the speakeasy. Shots were fired, a lot of them, then someone dove into the water, and the whole place exploded and caught fire.

So you can see, it was just another quiet night in Lake Wobegon, AKA, Canaveral Flats."

"Wow, you got shot at and lived," Marsha said.

"Glad it doesn't happen all the time. It's not something I think I could get used to."

"Anything else you can tell me?"

"There's more, but I need to keep it quiet for now," Roger said. "Say, have you seen Mr. Bracken in here lately?"

"Yeah, he was here yesterday, but he didn't seem to be his usual self. He's always quiet, but even more so yesterday. It seemed something was on his mind bothering him. I asked him if everything was okay and he said he might be leaving soon and not coming back. He seemed concerned, but also very determined."

"Like Julius Caesar at the Rubicon?"

"Yup, one of those kinds of looks. No turning back."

A voice cried out from the kitchen, "His breakfast is ready."

Marsha got up, went to the kitchen, and returned with his big breakfast. "Oh, sugar," she said. "Can't believe I forgot your coffee." She returned with a full pot and a cup. "Here you go. Anything else I can do for you?"

"How about a date?"

"Did I hear you right? You want to go on a date with me?"

Roger nodded. "I sure would. Catch a movie or something. Heard there's a new *Star Wars* movie out. Maybe take you out for a meal afterward, too."

"Any place but here. I spend half my life in this joint."

"It's a deal," Roger said. "Could you give me your phone number?"

"Just call the restaurant and ask for me," she said. "Roger, I'd like to talk more, but Cat needs my help in the kitchen preparing for the lunch crowd. Got to go. Looking forward to your call."

She smiled, turned, and disappeared into the kitchen.

Hungry Roger wolfed down the big breakfast. Maybe things were turning around for him. He had survived the night and would have a woman to talk to, something that had not happened in a year. Roger left a $10 bill on the table for the meal and tip and exited the building. He needed to take the plaster print to the coroner's office. Was it a match with the dead man's boot or not?

Chapter 29

Trickery and deception are common in nature, but the most deceptive creature of all is man. Unknown

One Week Later

It had been another hot week in Central Florida. A little rain had fallen, but it did little more than settle the dust. It would take a good soaking from a tropical storm or hurricane to break the drought. Roger was just finishing off his TV dinner and opened another can of beer when he saw Chief of Police Bill Kenney stop at the gate by the road, open it, and drive down the lane to Roger's trailer. K9, who was sleeping next to her bowl of dog food and water, opened one eye, growled, and went back to sleep. Roger said, "You still don't like him, but I think he may be growing on you. He's beginning to grow on me, but don't you tell him."

K9 sighed, and Roger said, "Good. Glad you agree with me." Bill exited his truck, walked to the porch, and entered. "Hey," Roger said. "Ya want a beer?"

"Why not? I'm off duty and got some things I need to talk with you about," Bill said. Roger handed a beer to Bill, who immediately opened it and chugged about half of it down. "Ain't nothing like a brewsky to quench a thirst on a hot as heck Florida evening. Hey Roger, you're usually drunk by now. What's up?"

"Well, ole buddy," Roger replied. "I've been doing a lot of thinkin'. I didn't think I was worth shootin' and somebody felt different. Guess I'm worth something after all. Changes my perspective somewhat." Roger continued, "The plaster of Paris mold

178

of the shoe prints at the spot where he shot at me matched the shoes the coroner took off the dead man we fished out of the river. We got the right guy. You know who he is yet?"

"Yeah, I have information on him. The FBI thinks he's a man known as the Stork. The coroner found a little stork-like tattoo on his chest over his heart. The picture Interpol sent was similar to our shooter. Coroner said he'd had some plastic surgery, but the ears matched. Most of the time, they change the face and not the ears. They're waiting on the fingerprint results to come back."

"Interpol and the FBI? This guy must be some kind of a seriously bad dude."

"He's been wanted for several assassinations on four continents. He's a serious killer and enforcer for an organization that they say doesn't exist, ODESSA. If he is the Stork, he has more aliases than Jimmy Carter has peanuts. They seemed unsure which one if any of them was his real name. Sounds like Tom set us on the right path."

"Wow, no wonder Bracken and the rabbi both warned me to be careful." Roger saw Bill down the last of his beer. "You want another one?"

"Sounds good to me," Bill said, and Roger handed Bill another beer. "If you're wondering about the body found in the ruins of Stiltsville, we have nothing. There wasn't much to ID on the charred remains, and since we don't know who it is, we cannot verify identity with dental charts. I'd say we've reached a dead end. All we know is a man's dead, and he had bullets in what wasn't consumed by the inferno."

"I wondered about Mr. Bracken. When I spoke to him, he always seemed to have more to say but held back. Still, don't know for sure where his loyalties were."

Bill said, "FYI, Randolph Valentine has disappeared. Rumor has it the State Department whisked him away to an undisclosed place outside of the United States. Right now, they won't deny or confirm anything about why he is absent from the space program, but you're free to connect the dots."

"Böse Menschen ungestraft bleiben."

"What's that mean?" Bill asked.

"It's something Tom said Werner von Braun had said," Roger replied. "Evil men go unpunished."

"It would sure seem that way," Bill lamented.

The two men said nothing for a moment. Roger broke the silence. "Got me a date."

"Why, you sly dog. With who?"

"Marsha, down at Umpa's."

"She is a fine-looking specimen of womanhood. What's she see in the likes of you?"

"Maybe she thinks there's still hope for me just like my wife did. Maybe she takes in strays. I don't know. Maybe she felt sorry for me. Whatever it was, I'm not goin' to screw it up."

"Have you decided to quit drinking yourself to death then?"

Roger was silent for a moment. "Last night, I tried. I walked out in my yard with a full bottle of Jack. I wanted so bad to pour it out, yet I couldn't. But I think I'm making some progress."

"I think so, too," Bill said. "Oh, the results on the bones the three of us dug up the day the pump died came back from the University of Florida Archaeological Dept. Their interpretation of the evidence is this; the two skulls we thought were old they dated at 6,000 to 8,000 years. The other skull with the bullet holes in it that was near the Civil War carbine gun, they dated at about 1870."

"Sounds like we have another suspicious death at Windover," Roger said.

"Yup, an extremely cold case. Think you might be interested in seeing what you could find on this one?"

Roger rubbed his chin. "Let me think on it for a while. Seems like after all this time, it can wait a few days or a week."

"I believe you're right," Bill said. "And on another point, the governor and the state legislature are still working on getting funding for an archaeological dig at the Windover site. It sounds like 'a go,' but you never know with those people. They did ask me to put out a feeler to you to see if you would like to be involved."

Roger smiled, "Yeah, I do have an interest in it. I'll have to wait and see what kind of an offer they make before I say yes or no.
"

"That's about what I thought you would say so I told them as much. I was trying to sweeten the pot for you."

"Bill, I appreciate all you have done for me."

"And, Roger, I couldn't have got this far without you."

"Thanks," Roger said.

Both men took a swig of beer and sat in the quiet with their own thoughts.

"I don't believe we've heard the last of this," Roger said.

Bill shook his head. "Me neither."

Chapter 30

As a man sows, shall he reap. And I know that talk is cheap. But the heat of the battle is as sweet as the victory. Bob Marley

Two weeks later. Oxapampa, Peru

The old man sat on the second-story porch of the Alpine-styled chalet nearly sleeping. The sun felt good on his shirtless chest. He looked down the deep, high jungle valley in the headwaters of the Amazon. He had crossed the bridge of no return, but it had been worth it. His escape had been carefully planned and had gone off with only one problem which he had used to his advantage.

He waited for the two men to return to Stiltsville late that night. From the heated argument they were having, he could tell it had not gone well, and the target had been missed. This pleased the old man. He had liked Roger Pyles from his first meeting. When the two men got into a gunfight, he was not surprised. Mistakes of this magnitude are not tolerated. He was amazed at the outcome. The Stork was slowing down, and it had pleased the old man when they shot each other down. All he had to do to finish the event was to cut the propane lines for the grills at the establishment and see it had caught fire when he slipped away in the water. The explosion was bigger than he had expected, but he dropped under the water as the heat and flame rolled over him.

He swam to the shore and walked to the used car lot where he had bought an old compact earlier in the week. The salesman was pleased to be paid in cash and had agreed to leave the car outside the gate for when he returned from his "vacation."

The busy Miami Airport was a four-hour drive away. A car could be left there for a long time without drawing attention. At the airport, he purchased a ticket to Mexico City and used a forged passport to fly to Panama on Copa Airlines. Another different forged passport was used for the flight to Lima, Peru. From there, it was an eight-hour car ride, even longer by the bus he took. The route took him over the desert coast and through the nearly 16,000-foot pass of Anticona in the high Andes, before dropping down to the lush central jungle at La Merced, and back up a death-defying climb to a high jungle valley where the town of Oxapampa, Peru is.

It was on the bus, his problem occurred. A dirty street urchin tried to steal his bag while he was catnapping. It had been a long time without sleep since he had escaped from Brevard County. A knife to the urchin's throat had produced an equally dirty man who claimed to be his father and begged him not to hurt the boy. He had agreed under the conditions that the father and son would be his eyes while he slept and in return, he would forget the hungry boy's indiscretion and pay the father two crisp new American twenty-dollar bills when they reached Oxapampa safely. He also gave them the snacks he had when he became ill from altitude sickness. The old man was very glad for their eyes at this time. As an added favor for a job well done, he gave them an additional twenty-dollar bill and told them to keep quiet which they readily agreed to do.

At the bus stop, he had found Humberto, a native to the area who spoke fairly decent English. Humberto had a tut-tut vehicle for hire. The old man quickly warmed to the young man as he showed him around the town of 10,000 in his rickshaw type vehicle. The old man had first heard of the village in an old tourist magazine at the Port St. John Library. He had been fascinated by the fact this forgotten village in the Andes was settled by Germans in the mid-1800s and still retained a German identity in its buildings and culture. Humberto took him to a restaurant he knew about which served Thuringian bratwurst, Döppekuchen potato flan, and the best beer the old man had tasted since leaving his homeland. He sampled some Camembert and Cambozola cheeses which melted in his mouth. He had found a place he could call home.

Humberto helped him find a chalet that first day. Since then, the young man would come every other day and show him more of the area. The old man was surprised to see a rodeo, coffee farms, and passion fruit orchards, but this was South America and not his native Bavaria. With the money he had at his disposal from skimming at

Stiltsville, he was set for life. He saw the familiar tut-tut coming up the country lane and stop in front of the chalet. "Humberto," he yelled. "Up here."

"Now I see you, Señor. I be up." He went into the chalet and soon appeared next to the old man on the porch. Señor, I see you enjoy our weather here. You are, soaking up some rays; I think they say."

The old man smiled. "Humberto, I see you have been watching American movies."

"The latest ones, Señor, *Beach Blanket Bingo*. So groovy."

The shirtless man laughed and said, "Young man, you never cease to amaze me."

At first, Humberto was not sure if he had said something that had been a faux pas but quickly realized the old man was laughing with him and not at him. Humberto laughed too.

"Señor, I did not know you had tattoo." He pointed to the old man's pink chest. "What kind of animal is it?"

"It's a little bear. The Americans would call it a teddy bear, but in my homeland, it's called a bracken."

"We call it here oso pequeno."

"That does kind of roll off your tongue. What do you have for me today?"

"I think I have found for you a maid."

"Good. Can she cook German meals?"

"Si, Señor. She work in past at Peruvian/German restaurant in town. She good cook."

"Can she cook too in the bedroom?"

"No, Señor. She is not that kind of woman."

"Good. Those are nothing but trouble."

"Si, Señor. Women are nothing except trouble."

"Can't live with them. Can't live without them."

"So true, Señor." He sighed. "But look. I have something for you. I find this newspaper in town, and it is in German. I read some first, but I not good in German. I think there is article about a famous German scientist who had died."

"Why thank you, Humberto." He took the newspaper from the young man. "I greatly appreciate your thoughtfulness. I believe I'm good for today." He handed the young man ten dollars.

"Thank you, Señor. I now be leaving, unless you need something else."

"I'm quite fine, Humberto. Bring the woman with you when you return in two days, and I'll have her make us a meal. See if she is as good as you say."

"She is better than I say, Señor."

"I'm sure she is. You've never led me wrong."

The young man nodded. "Goodbye Señor. Humberto entered the house, went down the stairs, and quickly disappeared in his tut-tut.

Enterprising young fellow that Humberto. He will go far. The man known as Bracken opened the newspaper and found the article the young man had seen. A smile came to his face. *This is interesting.*

***

The same day, Canaveral Flats, Florida, USA

Roger Pyles was napping in his new La-Z-Boy recliner when his ringing phone woke him.

"Hello," he said. "Whoever this is, you sure ruined a great dream."

"So sorry to wake you, Mr. Pyles, but I have important news for you."

"Yeah, like what? You want to sell me magazines, or maybe you're from that cemetery that keeps calling and trying to get me to buy a plot? Wants to make me a real permanent resident to the Sunshine State?"

"No, Mr. Pyles. The organization I am part of, and I would like to thank you for your tenacious work."

"Well, got to hand it to you, buddy, your approach is unique. Who are you, and what are you selling?" Roger growled.

"My name is Ehud Ben Gera, and I'm not trying to sell you anything. Do you have your *Florida Today* paper from yesterday?"

"I do, but I ain't read it yet."

"Please open it to page B4 and look at the article on the top."

"Okay, I'll bite. Let me see what your organization is selling in its ad. Okay, I'm tearing the wrapper off. Go to the B section.

Let's see, page 4." Roger looked at the article. A stunned look came to his face as he recognized the photograph of a man he had seen before.

"Are you there yet, Mr. Pyles?"

"Yeah, I'm there."

"Read it to me, please."

Roger started, "Randolph Valentine, former assistant director of NASA at Kennedy Space Center, was murdered in a suburb of Buenos Aires, Argentina late yesterday afternoon. Two men on a motorcycle pulled beside the car Valentine was riding in with a companion and sprayed the vehicle with automatic weapon fire. All in the car died. The assassins escaped and are still at-large. Police in Buenos Aires report the killers were possibly agents of Mossad, Israeli intelligence, known to be the world's most efficient killing machine. Valentine was rumored to have been part of the worst branch of the German SS, responsible for the deaths of millions of Jews during WWII. He had been living in Florida until a recent move to Argentina." Roger stopped reading. "Wow."

"So, Mr. Pyles, we want to thank you for your help in this matter. When he was under the protection of your government, our friend, we could not touch him, but because of you, the lion had to leave his den, and now he is our trophy. Thank you for your help. We could not have done it without you."

"You're welcome." The line went dead, and Roger sat stunned. "Böse Menschen sind schließlich bestraft" he whispered. "Evil men are finally punished." He paused to reflect. "And the dead still have tales to tell."

You write for two people, yourself and your audience who are usually better educated and at least as smart.   Tony Hillerman

WANT TO READ MORE?

Braddock's Gold Mystery Series

Braddock's Gold

Hunter's Moon

Fool's Wisdom

Killing Darkness

Florida Murder Mystery Series

Death at Windover

Murder at the Canaveral Diner

Murder at the Indian River

Murder at Seminole Pond

Murder of Cowboy Gene

Murder in the Family

WANT TO HELP THE AUTHOR?

If you enjoyed the book, would you help get the word out? Please tell others about it. Word-of-mouth advertising is the best marketing tool on this planet.

An honest review on Amazon, Goodreads, or elsewhere would help with the author being able to keep writing full time. It doesn't have to be long. Thanks.

SIGN UP FOR JAY HEAVNER'S NEWSLETTER

With this, Mr. Heavner will occasionally keep you informed with new books coming out and anything else special. Feel free to email him at jay@jayheavner.com. His website is www.jayheavner.com. He loves reader feedback. Thanks.